Praise for author's *Don*

2020 American Fiction Awards Winner in Family Saga and
Finalist in Women's Fiction

2020 International Book Awards Finalist in Historical Fiction

2020 National Indie Excellence Awards Finalist in Women's Fiction

2020 Next Generation Indie Book Awards Finalist in
General Fiction/Novel (Under 80k Words)

2019 Best Book Awards Finalist in Historical Fiction

"*Don't Put the Boats Away* is chock-full of well-researched historical details about political events, medical advancements, and even food trends of the 1940s, '50s, and '60s, and it also offers important commentary on professional opportunities for women during these decades. The author creates believable characters with complex interior lives. Overall, it's a touching tale that examines the ways in which grief, regret, and unmet expectations can reverberate through generations."

—*Kirkus Reviews*

"*Don't Put the Boats Away* is an impeccably researched and simultaneously heartfelt novel about what it was to be a woman and a scientist in the wake of the Second World War. The world needs more novels like this."

—Louisa Hall, *The Carriage House, Speak, Trinity*

Lemons
in the Garden
of Love

Lemons
in the Garden
of Love

a novel

Ames Sheldon

SHE WRITES PRESS

Published 2021
Printed in the United States of America
Print ISBN: 978-1-64742-048-2
E-ISBN: 978-1-64742-049-9
Library of Congress Control Number: 2020918232

For information, address:
She Writes Press
1569 Solano Ave #546
Berkeley, CA 94707

She Writes Press is a division of SparkPoint Studio, LLC.

This novel was inspired by and is dedicated to my great-grandaunt Blanche Ames Ames, a suffrage cartoonist, a cofounder of the Birth Control League of Massachusetts, a botanical illustrator and painter, an inventor, an architect, the wife of orchid expert Oakes Ames, and the mother of four.

To my fond imagination
Every woman in creation
Was a peach in
the Garden of Love

In its pleasant shade I wandered
Over my choice I slowly pondered
As I gazed at the branches above
All the peaches were so temptingly divine
That I couldn't see when I picked mine

Will someone kindly tell me
Will someone answer why
To me it is a riddle
And it will be till I die

A million peaches 'round me
Yes, I would like to know
Why I picked a lemon in
the Garden of Love

—M. E. Rourke

PROLOGUE

Smith College Library
Northampton, Massachusetts
August 1977

The naked woman on the cross shocks her. The woman's arms are stretched along a piece of wood, and her hands have been affixed to the ends. Her feet are in the process of being tied to a point near the bottom of the cross by someone whose back is turned to the viewer. The woman's large breasts hang pendulously, and her belly is gravid. She looks as though she is on the verge of delivering a baby. Off to the side, a man in a suit and top hat, smoking a cigar, stands next to someone else, and they appear to be discussing the woman. *What is this?*

Cassie leans closer to examine the drawing on the table before her. The woman's face has no features, and there isn't a signature anywhere on the piece. It appears to have been drawn with India ink on a heavy sheet of paper. It's so horrible she wants to look away, but she can't. The longer she gazes at it, the tighter her gut gets.

She was jolted by the electrifying image when she first saw it. This crucifixion was resting innocently in the middle of a folder labeled *K. R. E. Sketches*. It was probably drawn by Kate Reed Easton, a woman Cassie located in the card catalog at the Sophia Smith Collection. Cassie suspects that Kate Easton must be some sort of relative—Reed is her own middle name, and there are other Reeds in her mother's family. Why hasn't she heard of Kate Easton before? Though it's typical of her mother not to mention an ancestor—she doesn't care about history the way Cassie does.

Of course, it's possible that someone else drew this and Kate Easton kept it for some purpose. Cassie skims through the rest of the folder, but that's the only drawing of a woman on a cross.

Why would someone make a sketch like this? The artist would have needed a very pregnant woman to use as a model—if she even used a model. What is happening here? And who is the artist? There's so much to figure out. This is what Cassie loves about research: she feels like she's a detective pursuing clues to solve a mystery.

She has to stand up and walk around while her stomach flutters with excitement. Cassie had no idea what she'd find at Smith. The number of diaries and letters in the Kate Easton Collection is absolutely blowing her mind. Maybe she'll be able to do something with these materials.

The tall, double-hung windows nearby are so covered with ivy that the light slanting through seems nearly green. Fortunately, there's a brass lamp on the wooden table, which she turned on after requesting several archival Hollinger boxes from a staff member. Cassie came to Smith to see if she could get some ideas concerning a possible research topic for her doctoral dissertation. According to the archivist at the front desk, the Kate Easton Collection contains fifteen linear feet of items. If this drawing is any indication, the collection is very rich. What else is here, hiding in other folders?

But there's no way she'll be able to dig deep right now. The exhilaration that was rising in her turns to frustration when she considers the constraints on her time.

She sits down again. It's hot and stuffy in the archives, despite the high ceiling and the fans moving slowly nearby. Aside from the windows that fill one side of the room, the other walls are lined with shelves stuffed with books. Cassie pulls her sleeveless cotton blouse away from her chest where it has gotten stuck with sweat. She inches her skirt up above her knees. She only has two days in Northampton; the opportunity to leave Minnesota and come east arose suddenly ten days ago when her mother informed her that her sister Penny, who is pregnant, is getting married right away. There wasn't much time for Cassie to plan for this trip.

Why didn't Penny bother to call *her* about the news? Was she afraid Cassie would question her decision to get married? Now they all have to hustle to prepare for the event. Her sister hasn't even *talked* to her about the wedding, hasn't asked Cassie to stand up with her. That hurts. Penny was Cassie's maid of honor.

Tomorrow she'll take the bus back to Boston to catch up with her mother, who'll drive them out to Cape Ann. She'd much rather stay here in the library.

Actually, it's a thrill to be on her own for the first time in three years. Flaunting her freedom yesterday, she read *Fear of Flying* on the plane to Boston. She was struck by the anonymous quote on the first page: "Bigamy is having one husband too many. Monogamy is the same." She had to smile at that.

CHAPTER 1

Granite Cove, Massachusetts

"The Georges and the Thomases and the Petes—if they're there. And the Ben Juniors, we can't forget them."

Cassie adds these names to the list while her mother barrels her Oldsmobile station wagon down Route 128 at sixty-five miles per hour. She closes her eyes and savors the air streaming over her flushed face. It is cooler now, the farther they get from Boston. Then Cassie says, "My bus from Northampton had no air conditioning, and all the windows were jammed shut."

"Oh, add Cousin Susan and her new husband, what's-his-name."

"What *is* his name?"

"Nanny will know."

Cassie writes down "Cousin Susan plus?" Then she looks over at her mother. A breeze teases a tendril at Liz's right temple, but her sandy hair is too short to fly wantonly about. "Is Cousin Susan the first person to get divorced in our family?"

"Yep." Liz glances at Cassie. "Where are your glasses?"

"I'm wearing contacts. I hope I'll get used to them—"

"That's why you're squinting."

Thanks, Mom. Cassie knows she ought to be used to her mother's critical remarks, but she feels them anyway. Martin says she's simply too sensitive. She reaches over and turns on the radio, where "Go Your Own Way" is playing.

"And your hair—it's much more becoming when it's shorter."

Cassie replies coldly, "I like it longer."

Seemingly impervious to Cassie's tone, Liz says, "Your father and I will stay in the Bungalow with Nanny, so you'll be in charge at the Stone Lodge. Then we have the Cottage, and I've borrowed a couple of other houses from neighbors."

"Did you call the Bennetts?"

"They don't have room—Christopher's there for the summer."

Her high school boyfriend. Her first lover. *Is he married now?* She refocuses on her mother. "So, why didn't Dad come with you?"

"He'll drive up from Norwich Friday morning."

Cassie stares at the landscape streaming by. So much denser than the scenery back in Minnesota.

"Did you get the caterers?" Liz asks.

"What? I thought *you* already lined them up."

"I did. What I mean is, did you put them on the schedule for tomorrow?" Liz appears transfixed by a spot just beyond the top of the steering wheel.

Cassie shuffles through the lined yellow pages of the notepad. "It's here. Of course it is." Her mother is eminently capable of handling the preparations for Penny's wedding, even on such short notice. "Have you met the Roses yet? I can't believe Penny's marrying into a family we've never met."

Liz replies brusquely, "I'll be meeting them this weekend, just like you." She sighs. "Now, if we start with clams Friday night, chicken casserole will be good enough for dinner, won't it?"

"Chicken casserole for the bridal dinner? That's not very festive."

As a newlywed, Cassie's first experience cooking dinner from scratch was a disaster. She'd crumpled a dozen bay leaves into tomato sauce before simmering, and the result gave her and Martin such bad stomach aches that from then on, she followed recipes religiously, trying a new one from the Grand Diplôme cooking course each week. It was a way she thanked him for paying their bills.

"Well, this isn't the Waldorf Astoria. We're at the beach, after all. Chicken will be fine."

"You have everything under control, Mom. As usual."

Liz punches the cigarette lighter in and reaches for the pack on the seat next to her. Once she lights her Salem, she inhales and then exhales a stream of smoke.

A drop of sweat slides down between Cassie's breasts. "It is so hot. Have you heard the forecast for the weekend?"

"No, why bother?" Slowing for the exit, Liz scowls at an old Rambler creeping in front of her. "There's not much we can do about the weather."

Cassie pulls out her Marlboros and pushes the lighter back in.

As soon as she reaches the rotary, Liz swings around the Rambler and takes the last turnoff; now they are on a narrow road that meanders along the coast.

"Mom, at Smith yesterday, I was digging around in the Sophia Smith Collection for my dissertation. I found diaries that belonged to Kate Reed Easton."

Liz replies, "One of Nanny's aunts. I didn't know her well. You can ask Nanny about her."

"I *thought* we must be related! While I was doing research on suffrage earlier this summer, I came upon a cartoon by Kate Easton that President Taft denounced in the *Saturday Evening Post*. Once I got to Smith, I looked for material about her, and I found a whole lot of stuff, but I had no idea her middle name was Reed. Did you know she drew suffrage cartoons? The librarian said—"

"Remind me to call the liquor store." Liz threads the car through a small, unmarked driveway flanked on both sides by a low granite wall.

Cassie flips her cigarette butt out the window, annoyed. "Did you hear what I said?" She snaps off the radio, just as James Taylor starts to sing "Your Smiling Face."

"I'm not interested in all that ancient history." Liz is concentrating on the potholes in the skinny lane that weaves through the woods. "What time does Martin's flight get in tomorrow?"

"Just before noon."

"Give me the details so your father can pick him up at the airport on his way out here."

The car reaches an open field of grass. As soon as Liz pulls to a stop, she says, "Nanny has lunch for us. You can get your stuff later."

Once Cassie steps out of the car, she is assailed by the expanse of space and light. She hasn't been back to Granite Cove since the summer before she and Martin married. Blue sky and sea, only a shade of color separating them, reflect each other all the way to the horizon. A bell buoy in the middle of the bay rocks gently with the waves; a few sailboats shift on their moorings. Cassie circles slowly, taking it all in. Liz strides toward the Bungalow, forcing her daughter to scramble to catch up to her.

Nanny throws open the door. "At last!"

"Oh, Nanny," says Cassie warmly, "it's so good to see you!"

Nanny places her hands on Cassie's arms and bends forward so their upper torsos meet. She kisses Cassie's cheek and steps back. "How nice that you could come help your mother with the wedding."

Her grandmother's smile is as sweet as ever, but the change in her appearance shocks Cassie. Nanny has lost at least ten pounds since the memorial service last winter. She even seems shorter.

"Would you two like iced tea, or something stronger? I'm having a Heineken. Help yourself, Cassie. Liz, come sit with me."

Her mother says, "Tea for me, Cassie."

Cassie enters the room that serves for living, dining, and cooking.

Usually she sees Nanny at her home in New Jersey, so she'd forgotten how small and cozy her grandmother's summer cottage is.

She can hear her mother on the porch now, saying, "Everyone over fifty gets a chair for the bridal dinner. The bride and groom and the rest of the class B adults can eat on their laps. I'm not going to worry about children. Their mothers can take care of them."

Cassie finds glasses on one of the open shelves in the tiny kitchen. After she pours the tea, she heads toward the porch but pauses at the door a moment to observe her mother and grandmother through the screen. Nanny has her back to the sun as she looks at the water. Her mouth droops a little. Liz scratches something off one of her lists. Then she says, "I've got to decide whom to put at the Inn. Aunt Lydia, for one. I bet she'd like someplace quiet where she can hide from the action. What about the Griffins, Mummy?"

Startled, Nanny looks confused. "Oh, I don't expect them to come."

Cassie opens the screen door. Handing a glass to her mother, she takes the chair next to Nanny. "Class B?"

Liz replies, "Adults of your generation. Class As are my generation and older."

"That's a new one. You're so organized, Mom. I admire that."

Liz brushes the air with her hand, dismissing the compliment.

Cassie crosses her legs, hooking the right around the left, cocking her right foot at the ankle so the arrangement won't slip. Then she notices that her mother is sitting in the same position. She smiles to herself.

Nanny says, "I'm just sorry Matt won't be here; you'd think he'd want to be part of his sister's wedding."

Liz shakes her head. "I couldn't even reach Matt to let him know. He's somewhere in the depths of Bulgaria working on an archaeological dig with his advisor. Now, Mummy, about the service. Penny told me she and Steven want it on the lawn in front of the Lodge. How many chairs do you think we should set up?"

"I don't know. How many people have you invited?" Then, sounding querulous, "I don't see how you can feed so many people without more help! What are you thinking?"

"We've already gone over that, Mother." In the noon glare, Liz looks a little faded, her hair a dustier red, her freckles slightly fainter. Cassie wishes she had red hair like her mother and sister rather than this mouse-brown mop. There's no point in worrying about her looks, but sometimes she can't help herself.

"I'm following Penny and Steven's wishes," Liz explains. "They want to be 'informal.' That's why we're having the wedding at Granite Cove. Of course, venues we might have considered when we started making calls were booked ages ago—"

"Oh," Nanny says, "I meant to tell you. The caterers called. They'll be here at nine tomorrow. If that doesn't suit you, you'd better call them back. Cassie, the tuna is ready in the icebox, the bread's in the breadbox. Would you put it all together? I only want a half—"

"Mummy, you've got to eat. Half a sandwich isn't enough—"

"I'm not hungry, Liz."

"Nanny," Cassie says to defuse the rising tension, "what can you tell me about Kate Reed Easton? She was one of your aunts?"

"My mother's sister. She was a colorful character—a suffragette."

"A suffra*gist*," corrects Cassie. Liz rolls her eyes.

"And she worked tirelessly for birth control," says Nanny. "If only Penny . . ."

Liz says, "I just hope Penny knows what she's doing. Steven is quite—"

Cassie interrupts, "No one cares that he's Jewish, Mom."

"That's not what I mean. Make the sandwiches, Cassie," says Liz. "Give us each a whole one."

"Yes, sir," replies Cassie. She retreats to the kitchen. She pulls out the bag of white Pepperidge Farm bread and places it on the table. Then she opens the refrigerator. There isn't much inside, other than several bottles of Heineken, Coleman's mustard and Heinz ketchup, some lemons and a shriveled lime, along with Hellman's mayonnaise and the bowl of tuna fish. As she assembles the ingredients, she thinks about the fact that at home with Martin she's always the one to make the sandwiches. She should tell him to do it occasionally.

When she brings the platter out to the porch, Nanny asks, "Did you know *I* marched in a birth control parade?"

"You did?"

"I must have been about eighteen or nineteen—it was after the Great War. Aunt Kate was trying to swell the ranks with as many bodies as she could enlist. She convinced Mother to bring us all along."

"Did you know this, Mom?"

Liz shakes her head.

"That must have been very exciting, Nanny!"

"The only thing I remember is my loose knickers," says Nanny. "I'd lost a button and they kept sliding down, so I had to keep hauling them back up."

Cassie and Liz chuckle at the image of Nanny, the archetype of propriety, wrestling with her underwear in public.

"It certainly wasn't amusing at the time," Nanny responds dryly. "Birth control was not popular, not like it is now. There're lots of Catholics in Boston. They threw eggs and garbage at us."

"You're kidding! What did you do?"

"I don't remember. I suppose we just kept marching. But that's long ago, and now, it's time for my nap." Abruptly, Nanny stands and, without another word, walks into the house.

Cassie and Liz exchange a look. Cassie asks softly, "Is Nanny OK? She enjoyed talking about that march, but then she cut the conversation off."

"Nanny is doing as well as can be expected."

"She must miss Grandpa terribly."

"I'm sure she does. The wall between our rooms is so thin I hear her crying at night, but she doesn't want to talk about him. If I mention Father's name, she flinches."

Cassie sighs. While she collects the glasses and plates, Liz picks up the dirty ashtrays and opens the door. Both women pause to adjust to the relative gloom inside. After emptying the ashtrays into the trash, Liz says, "I'm worried about your father."

"Why? What's happening?"

"Over the weekend, see if you can find out what's bothering him. He's been coming to bed later and later, which is fine by me, but he seems a little lost."

"What do you mean?"

"He's taken to wandering around, looking for people to talk with. Aside from writing his weekly sermon, he doesn't have enough to do anymore."

"Is that because of the new minister the board hired?"

"I don't know, Cassie. He says everything's fine, but I can see that's not true. Maybe he'll talk to you."

"How long has this been going on?"

"I can't keep track of every little thing." Liz sounds angry now. "I've got a wedding to worry about."

"Is anything wrong with him physically?"

"Not that he's said."

"I hate to think Dad isn't his usual self. I'll ask him."

Liz turns toward the stairs. "I'm going up now too."

"I want to get some sun. Are there any outdoor jobs to be done right now?"

Liz stops, one leg flexed on the first step. "Why don't you take a look at the Cottage and see what we need down there. Those beds have to be made up, but it's much easier with two . . . never mind, we can do that together when I get up. Do whatever you want now. You'll be plenty busy later on."

Barefoot, Cassie steps on the tan pathway stones, taking care to avoid the black rocks, which are painfully hot on a day like this. Finally, she reaches the beach. A light breeze pricks her nostrils as she faces the sea. Not far offshore, a sailboat leans into a new tack. The movement of the water seems to call to her blood.

She wraps her arms around herself as she walks across the sand. It's a relief to spend a few days by herself, away from Martin for the first time since their wedding. After a while she stops and stands in place, shifting her weight from one foot to the other, creating little bogs. When she is ankle-deep, she spots a particularly auspicious hole and leans over to dig for the probable clam, though several inches down she finds nothing. Once Cassie and her cousins were so adept at locating quahogs that they depleted the beach. Apparently, the clam population hasn't recovered yet.

A door slams. The woman who emerges from the Cottage and begins to rake the grass works so steadily and smoothly she might be thirty-five, not fifty-three.

Cassie crosses the sand to her. "I see how you stay in shape, Aunt Grace."

"Cassie!" Grace drops her rake. "*Good* to see you."

"Word is you've made improvements to the Cottage since I was last here."

"Let me show you." She leads the way inside, pointing out new sliding glass doors, re-covered cushions, and a colorful straw rug in the living room.

Cassie moves over to the bookcase set against the far wall. Stooping, she skims the spines of the dog-eared paperbacks. When she pulls out a hardback copy of *The Wind in the Willows*, it flops open to the flyleaf, where "Grace, Happy Christmas from Father, 1933" is inscribed. She hands the open volume to her aunt, who grimaces.

Grace replaces the book. "Now," she says, "you must see the pièce de résistance."

Grace takes Cassie through the small dining room and the kitchen, double its former size, to the back room. Once the most cramped of the bedrooms, the babysitter's room has been expanded by several feet in each direction, and it features a huge picture window overlooking the bay.

"I don't know what came over me," says Grace. "It's completely impractical to have a house so close to the ocean with a wall of glass facing the water like this, but I couldn't resist, the view is so great."

"This is *wonderful*, Aunt Grace," says Cassie, sitting on the queen-size bed.

Grace settles down beside her.

"When I was at Smith yesterday, I found some diaries written by Kate Reed Easton. Did you know Aunt Kate?"

"Not terribly well. I believe she went to Smith. I remember spending some time with Aunt Kate and Uncle Del at their house down the road from here. It was basically just a studio. She was a remarkable woman in many ways. An excellent portrait painter. Your mother and I would model for her when she needed someone to pose."

"Far out! What else can you tell me about her?"

"As a child, I thought she and Uncle Del were a little scary. Sometimes they'd invite Liz and me to dinner—they were intimidating because they put such grown-up questions to us. Once she asked me if I found Van Gogh unsettling. No doubt they were trying to engage us in conversation. I just felt dumb. They didn't know how to talk to children since they had none of their own. I never knew why. She seemed to like children well enough. She lived in Paris for a while, if I recall correctly. Ask Nanny; she'll know more." Standing, Grace says, "I should get back to my raking now. You know my husband keeps me jumping. Rick will be coming back here with me tomorrow. How is your nice husband?"

"Martin's fine. Coming tomorrow, too. Are you joining us for dinner tonight?"

"Yes. See you later, Cassie. And remember, here at Granite Cove the cocktail hour starts at six!"

Cassie carries her suitcase and L.L.Bean bag stuffed full of books and papers into the Stone Lodge and up the concrete stairs to the second story. She continues down the long hall to the master bedroom, opens the windows wide, and then quickly unpacks, hanging two dresses in the closet, shoving underwear, shirts, and shorts into a chest of drawers. She sets her toilet articles on a table outside the tiny bathroom. After changing into a tie-dyed T-shirt and cut-off jeans, she arranges a pillow between her back and the headboard, stretches out her legs on the double bed, and opens the folder containing the Xeroxes. At Smith she had to race through Kate's daily diaries, flagging those entries that caught her eye, so the staff could make copies of those pages for her to take away. She hopes she spotted the most important entries.

Last night Cassie had a dream in which she and Kate were both driving very fast. Kate's car was right behind Cassie's and she was calling out to Cassie, trying to convey an urgent message, but Cassie couldn't figure out what Kate was saying. What was Kate trying to tell her?

September 1, 1912: Today I met an intriguing man named Del Easton, who is an assistant professor in botany at Harvard College. I get the impression that he has sufficient family wealth that he does not need to work, but he has such an inquiring mind that he must be well suited for a scientific profession. He asked many questions and listened carefully to my replies before following up with other precise queries, but when I directed inquiries to him, he responded very briefly. I think he must be quite shy. He has a silly sense of humor, which I like—he's really quite endearing.

November 9, 1912: Earlier this evening at the home of one of Del's colleagues from the botany department, I became embroiled in a heated discussion of Thorstein Veblen and his *Theory of the Leisure Class*. The man enrages me. Veblen does not value women in the least—he considers us to be parasites. Veblen would consign me to the ranks of leisure-class women, but my purpose in life is neither conspicuous consumption nor profligate spending. I don't waste my time in trivial pursuits. I am much more serious—as are many other women Veblen neglects to consider in his book. I believe the difficulty lies in men who are too theoretical; their theories omit all the particularities of actual experience.

While driving me home, Del said he was surprised by the bitterness I displayed. He explained that Veblen is a satirical writer; in reading Veblen literally, I missed the point.

I saw immediately that Del was right—which silenced me at the time—but now as I think things over, I feel angrier than ever. I grant that satire can enable the reader to apprehend something in a new light, but it also allows the author to avoid making any sort of constructive statement. I comprehend what Veblen is *against* but not what he stands *for*.

February 14, 1913: Del asked me to marry him this evening. I told him that I would think about his proposal. He is a fascinating companion, and over these past months we have discovered many shared sympathies and beliefs. I was touched by the hesitant way in which he expressed his devotion, but I confess that I had to suppress a smile when he told me he had waited expressly for Saint Valentine's Day before declaring himself. (I would not have suspected sentimentality from such a rational scientist.)

Del travels far and wide in pursuit of rare ferns, which is his area of special expertise, and I wonder how I would feel being left alone for weeks at a time. I will need to consider that.

Meanwhile, I know that I must divulge a complete account of my history, even though it may lead him to change his mind about marrying a woman with my experience.

Cassie puts the pages down. Del proposed to Kate after knowing her for—she tallies quickly—six months? Was that typical in the 1910s? For her and Martin, it was only four months between the time she started working at Faegre and Whitney and his proposal. Should she have gotten to know him better before she said yes? What does Kate mean by "a woman with my experience"?

February 16, 1913: Del and I discussed his travels. His trips generally take him away for at least two weeks at a time, and sometimes they last as long as several months. He assured me I should not be lonesome since we would be living at his home—his mother and I would have each other for companionship.

Then I told Del everything about Paris and asked him to consider whether that information changes his feelings for me. Now I await his decision. I hope he will not judge me too harshly, but if he does, then he is not the right husband for me.

February 17, 1913: Last evening Del's opening words were that he respected me for confiding in him. He reiterated his love for me and his desire that I consent to become his wife.

I said that I will marry him. My affection for Del continues
to grow. He is absolutely solid and reliable, he is kind, and he
loves me dearly. I know that my mother likes him, although
Evelyn is skeptical because I do not exhibit the girlish glee
that she expects in one who is becoming betrothed. I told
my sister that I do not feel all thrilly in Del's presence, but I
am no schoolgirl in the throes of a crush. I trust I shall never
again forget myself with any man. I am attracted to Del, and
at the same time I don't believe I will lose myself in him. His
physical appearance is pleasing to me, even though he is not
handsome. In fact, he is so tall and lanky that he reminds me
a little of Ichabod Crane—I don't think I shall ever tell him
that. Being with Del makes me feel calm and safe and happy.

We will marry soon after he returns from his expedition
to Costa Rica, a country with three times as many species
of fern as the United States and Canada. I look forward to
the adventure of creating a new life in partnership with this
intriguing man.

Did Kate fall desperately in love with some man she knew in
Paris? What happened? Was he married? Cassie knows what Kate
means by "losing herself." She lost herself to a guy in college, couldn't
resist him. She'd do just about anything he wanted until she found
out he had other girlfriends. She vowed she'd never let herself get
carried away again. She had accepted Martin's proposal because they
had similar interests and he's very bright. That, and she was about to
turn twenty-three. All her friends were settling down.

CHAPTER 2

At six, Nanny is sitting on her front porch in a cotton print dress and white shoes, her hands in her lap. Liz, Grace, and Cassie join her, holding glasses of whiskey, wine, and Coke, respectively. Cassie enjoys a gin and tonic every now and then, but she's much less of a drinker than the other women.

"It's a treat not to have to drink alone," says Nanny, surveying her daughters and granddaughter. She swirls the ice in her Canadian Club for emphasis.

The other women are dressed in skirts for dinner, since that is one of Nanny's rules.

"Just us women," Cassie announces, thinking of the women's group she joined last year. It's the only thing she does outside of school and marriage because when she started taking an exercise class at the Y, Martin complained about her being gone two evenings a week. "I have an idea, ladies. Recently I became a member of a consciousness-raising group in Minneapolis, which I really like."

"What is that?" Nanny asks.

"It's women sitting together in a circle. Someone asks a personal question, and then everyone answers from her own point of view."

Grace says, "What kind of questions, Cassie?"

"Something like everyone giving an example from her own life about how she has experienced oppression as a woman."

"That could be interesting," Grace replies.

"Sounds like a waste of time," says Liz.

Cassie suggests, "How about this question: Do you hope Penny's baby will be a boy or a girl?"

Nanny says, "A girl. Girls stay closer to their mothers."

"Boys have more opportunities," Grace remarks.

Liz says, "This is a ridiculous exercise. I don't see the point."

Cassie explains, "When we talk about our personal feelings and discover our commonalities as women, it can be very empowering."

Liz insists, "Let's get back to business."

"All right, Mom." Reaching for her mother's yellow pad, Cassie asks, "Nanny, what's the name of Cousin Susan's new husband?" She's had plenty of practice being a dutiful daughter; sometimes there is comfort in playing that role.

"I can't remember. I haven't met him yet."

"They live in the Boston area, don't they?"

Liz says, "I'll call Susan in the morning."

Picking up her pack of Marlboros from the side table, Cassie says, "Nanny, I've been reading some papers I found at Smith. About Kate Easton. How old did Aunt Kate get to be?" She lights a cigarette and exhales the smoke.

"Aunt Kate? She died years ago—I'd have to look up the exact date."

"Would you please, Nanny?"

"Then bring me the book. I think it's on the shelf above the Franklin stove."

Cassie fetches the family records, a mimeographed volume of seventy-five pages covering fifteen generations from the arrival of John Reed at the Bay Colony in 1638.

Grace says, "Oh, *that* book! The earliest information is sketchy, but the generations since the Civil War are carefully chronicled. Full details of births, deaths, marriage, and children."

Nanny flips through a number of pages before replying. "This says she died in 1970, so she would have been over eighty."

"Did I ever meet her?" Cassie asks, turning to her mother. "I don't remember her. Her husband—Del—was a botanist."

Liz, busy making notes on her yellow pad, does not respond.

Nanny frowns at Liz. "You may not have met her, Cassie," she says, putting down the book. "After Uncle Del died, Aunt Kate spent all her summers in the Studio until she fell and hurt her back—she kept a very low profile after that."

"Mummy," Grace interjects, "how did you get the Cottage?"

"My mother and her sisters traded houses when they saw the way the family was growing. Mother already had the Stone Lodge, so she took these two houses next to the Lodge. Aunt Kate built the Studio. Cousin Jessie acquired a couple of houses up the hill, and Cousin Gertie had a place down the road toward Annisquam."

"The women decided it all?" says Cassie. "Interesting. What about their husbands?"

Liz impatiently riffles through the lists on her lap.

Unperturbed, Nanny replies, "Husbands didn't have a lot to say about it. They made up a club of their own. They even had an emblem, a lemon fastened on a white silk ribbon, from some popular song about lemons in the garden of love."

"I've never heard of that song."

"Oh, it's an old one. Something about the women being peaches in the garden of love. I think the men must have been the lemons."

"This is so matriarchal," says Cassie. "What about brothers—didn't your mother and the other aunts have brothers or sons?"

"Yes, but most of them didn't spend much time around here, and they certainly didn't bother to build their own houses nearby. They borrowed their mothers'. Thomas is the only exception I can think of."

"Can we get back to work now?" Liz flourishes the cigarette in her long, elegant fingers. "I'd like to run through the schedule for the weekend to make sure everything's straight."

As she details the plans for the wedding, Cassie is struck once again by how much her mother loves being in charge. When Cassie got engaged, she was working in Minnesota, so Liz handled all the arrangements for her wedding at their family home in Connecticut three years ago. She's pondering the parallels between preparing for a wedding and a military campaign when Liz's voice breaks through. "Quiches and cold cuts sound perfect for lunch on Saturday, Grace, but won't that be an awful lot of work for you?"

"Actually," Grace says, "I have twenty-five quiches in my freezer right now."

"Why would you have so many, Aunt Grace?"

"Rick and I miscommunicated. I thought he wanted me to make enough quiches to provide brunch for the class celebrating its twenty-fifth reunion at Governor Dummer. I was wrong." Rising, she asks, "Anyone want a refill?"

Cassie collects glasses and follows her aunt into the house. As they refresh everyone's drinks, Grace whispers, "Isn't Mummy doing well? I'm so proud of her."

Cassie says, "Don't you think it's liberating for Nanny to be free after all these years? Grandpa was such a formidable man." Then it occurs to her that she's imagining how she might feel after sixty years of marriage to Martin.

"Oh no," Grace asserts, "that's not freedom. Besides, Mummy has always done pretty much as she likes."

"What is freedom, then?" With all the expectations emanating from her husband, Cassie worries that she'd no longer recognize it.

"Nothing I'd ever want. Life is hardly worth living if you're all alone."

"To me," Cassie says, "freedom means being your own person, living your life your own—"

From the porch Liz calls, "Turn the heat all the way up under the big pot of water, will you?"

"Sure," Cassie replies, and she does as she's told. Rejoining the women on the porch, she asks, "Does that water mean what I think it does?"

"You bet—we're having lobsters. You can't come all the way from Minnesota and not eat a lobster," Liz says, smiling.

"That's great! Thank you, Mom."

"I picked them up at the fish market this afternoon," Nanny says. "I was shocked to see they cost $2.99 a pound now."

"The price was higher than that in June," says Grace, taking her seat. "Will you please pass the peanuts, Cassie?"

Nanny watches a ladybug that landed on her arm. "Ladybug, ladybug," she croons. "Fly away home, your house is on fire, your children will burn." She flings the bug into the air, staring after it, her eyes brimming with tears.

"Why don't we get dinner going?" Liz stands. Grace and Cassie both jump up. Grace moves to touch her mother's shoulder, but Nanny waves her off. They leave Nanny alone to pull herself together.

Inside, Liz opens the window over the sink. As Grace reaches for the salad bowl, Cassie says, "Wouldn't Nanny feel better if she could talk about missing Grandpa?"

Grace says, "I should think so."

"You can't make Mummy do anything she doesn't want to do," Liz comments. Then she hauls the lobsters out of the refrigerator and removes them from the paper bag. She plunges the lobsters, one by one, headfirst into the boiling water and seaweed.

Cassie goes upstairs to use the bathroom, then tiptoes into Nanny's bedroom and sits gingerly on the large bed that fills most of the space. A photo of her grandfather stands on the little table next to one side. It's Cassie's favorite; it shows him in a dark suit, a straw hat, and the white tennis shoes he always wore. *I do not feel all thrilly in Del's presence.* Kate's words come back to Cassie and she wonders, *Did Nanny feel "thrilly" with Grandpa?*

When Cassie rejoins her mother and aunt downstairs, Nanny pushes open the screen door, saying, "I don't know what it is about twilight. Lately the end of the day makes me blue."

"Understandable, Mummy," says Grace. "I often feel blue at this time of day."

Nanny shakes her head. Then she says, "What a nice job you've all done setting the table, and that salad looks good. Where did the flowers come from?"

Liz pulls out a chair for her mother. "Grace brought them from her garden. Aren't they nice, Mummy?"

"Beautiful. They certainly dress up the table. Would you light the candles, Cassie? And then I want you to sit next to me."

They crack open their lobsters and begin to eat. Cassie says, "I'm probably getting way ahead of myself, but I've started thinking about a topic for my dissertation. I've been studying for my preliminary written and oral exams all summer, and I have to pass them before I present my research proposal, and of course that has to be original work for me to earn a doctorate."

Dipping a lobster claw into a small china cup of melted butter, Liz says, "Tell Nanny about your paper."

"My master's thesis. I was looking at the women's hospital groups that began to spring up in the 1870s. I believe those auxiliaries served a genuinely radical function. They gave women an acceptable reason to leave their homes and spend time working together for the benefit of the ill—who fall within the traditional sphere of women's concerns, so it was OK—but what *really* happened was that a large group of women learned organization and management skills, and for the first time they saw they could be effective in the public sphere. They developed a sense of self-confidence that helped pave the way for the suffrage movement."

"That's interesting," Nanny replies. "I know I enjoyed working with the Red Cross during the Second World War."

"Women have always had organizational skills," Liz asserts. "We have to if we want to keep our husbands, households, and children in order."

"Aunt Kate worked on behalf of the New England Hospital for Women and Children," Nanny adds. "She gave them financial support, too."

"When was this?"

"In the forties, I believe."

"I'm so glad I found her diaries," Cassie continues, "though the problem doing research like mine is how can you know what people were thinking one hundred years ago? It's a question that fascinates me."

"You can tell what people were thinking from what they wrote," Grace replies.

"Letters and diaries help, but they don't necessarily reveal a person's innermost thoughts. People in the nineteenth century had a highly developed sense of privacy."

"I never kept a diary," Nanny says.

"This is so much fun," Cassie exclaims. "I love being able to talk about things like this with you all."

"I like hearing what you're up to," Nanny answers.

"I'm glad, Nanny." Cassie pauses to light a cigarette. Then she asks, "Aunt Grace said Aunt Kate lived in Paris for some time?"

"I believe she studied art there before she married. That's all I can tell you," Nanny answers. She hoists the bottle of merlot and pours herself some more. "Cassie, with all this research, how do you find the time to take care of Martin?"

"He's pretty good at taking care of himself."

"You mustn't take anything for granted. Hold on tight to your husband. You wouldn't believe how much you'll miss him when he's gone." In the candlelight, her eyes glisten.

Not knowing what to reply to that, Cassie puts her cigarette down and reaches for her Coke.

Grace says, "I was excited when Liz told me about Penny's pregnancy—the next generation! And don't worry, I'm not telling anyone—not even Rick. What about you, Cassie? When do you and Martin plan to start a family?"

Brusquely, she replies, "Not till after I finish my dissertation. Then we'll see."

"Since you didn't change your name when you and Martin married, what last name will you give your kids? Would it be Lyman-Matas?"

"I've wondered about that too," murmurs Nanny.

Crushing her cigarette in the ashtray, Cassie crosses her arms in front of her chest. "I have no idea."

"Ah," Grace replies. "Well, I'm sorry my boys can't make it to the wedding. They're in their last weeks of summer camp. Percy's a counselor this summer."

"Is he enjoying that?" Nanny asks.

"Absolutely. After four years at Camp Kieve, he's pleased to have a job at the place he loves."

"Matt won't be here either," Liz says. "He's still in Bulgaria."

Grace continues, "What kind of dress will Penny be wearing?"

Liz replies, "My wedding dress. We had it shortened—now it's tea length."

"What about you, Cassie?" Grace inquires.

"I'm not in the wedding," Cassie says coolly. She wishes Aunt Grace would stop asking annoying questions. "What is Uncle Rick doing this summer? He must get a lot of time off when Governor Dummer's not in session."

"Not really. Summer's the time administrators catch up with everything they've had to put off during the school year. Speaking of which, Rick will be wondering where I am; I'd better get on the road back to Byfield." She glances at her watch. "It's already nine-thirty!" She clears her place and begins to collect her things.

"Oh, it's too early for you to go, Grace! Won't you drink some coffee first?" asks Liz. "Or Sanka?"

"Thanks, no, Liz, I'll take off. See you nice people tomorrow." She kisses Nanny on the cheek. "Goodnight, Mummy. Goodnight, all."

Once Grace is out the door, Liz comments, "She looks so scrawny; hasn't she been eating?"

"Personal remarks," warns Nanny.

"All right, Mother. How about dessert?"

"We don't have any."

"There's lemon yogurt in the Lodge," Cassie offers. "I'd be glad to get it."

"Yogurt!" Nanny scoffs. "I don't understand you children and your health foods. Vegetarianism, too! I haven't had yogurt since your grandfather and I were in Greece thirty years ago. I don't plan to start now."

"Fine, no yogurt," Liz replies. "Let me make you a Sanka, Mummy. And you, too, Cassie. Do you want to move over to the couch?"

Nanny says, "I'm going to bed. You can do as you please. Shut the windows before you come up, Liz. It's so chilly in the morning if they're open all night."

"Sure, Mummy."

"Thanks for a lovely evening, Nanny. Sleep well."

"Night," Liz calls when Nanny is halfway up the stairs. Then she slumps in her chair, looking beat. "I think I've done enough for one day. Unless you want a hand?"

Cassie is sliding the empty lobster shells back into the stockpot. "No, Mom, you relax. I'll finish up. Is Nanny really all right?"

"She's fine. You know—she hates people fussing over her. She'd much rather be the one taking care of everyone else." Liz rises, pats her daughter's forearm, and leaves the room.

—

After dumping the lobster shells in the trash can out in the Bungalow shed and washing the dishes, Cassie starts up to bed. She can hardly wait to remove her contact lenses—her eyes aren't used to them. As she pulls her nightgown over her head, she decides she's not going to call Martin. He's probably still at the office anyway. She respects the ambition and drive he has—she's not going to interfere with his work. Meanwhile, she wants to know what happened next with Kate.

<u>May 24, 1913</u>: Ever since I finished reading *Julia France and Her Times* last night, the novel has preoccupied my thoughts. I cannot fathom why Gertrude Atherton should insist there exists a "war between the sexes" that governs all of our relations. I disagree. I never received an impression of any struggle between my parents, and Del and I have such high regard and respect for one another that we never argue—I cannot imagine that will change with marriage.

According to *Julia France,* the battle of the sexes is a clash that occurs inevitably between men and women. Ibsen suggests the same. Is there some truth here that I am missing? Men and women certainly differ in their moral qualities and in their susceptibility to emotion, but to hold that men and women must be unalterably opposed is too disconcerting a thought. If I believed that, I could not marry anyone.

I wonder why I should feel so frightfully troubled by this. Perhaps I am experiencing a case of prenuptial nerves? Truly there is no good reason for me to worry.

Del recognizes that a wedding ring can be construed as a sign of bondage, so instead he is giving me a perfectly beautiful sapphire-and-diamond necklace. What a dear man! He comprehends what women face when they marry.

For him, I have found a very fine magnifying glass that

dangles on a gold chain, which I will present to him at our wedding supper. I trust that he will use this glass every day for the rest of his life.

Cassie looks at the plain gold band on her left hand. It chafes at times, but whenever she removes it to apply cream on the sore part of her finger, Martin makes a comment. It certainly feels like a symbol of bondage. At least she didn't give up her own last name when they married.

CHAPTER 3

"I'm looking to see if she's awake, Mom!"

Cassie's eyes pop open at the sound of Penny's voice. The room is swimming in sunshine.

Penny sticks her head around the door, bounds onto Cassie's bed, and gives her a big hug. "How's my lazy big sister?" she teases. "You planning to get up?"

"Why would I? Apparently, you don't need me for anything," Cassie replies.

"I'm sorry, Cassie. I meant to call you to tell you we were getting married, but then I got all caught up in the details with Mom and . . . well, you know what she's like."

Penny looks so happy that Cassie can't stay angry at her. They were so close, once upon a time, sleeping in the same room, sharing secrets. Sliding her legs out from under the covers, she says, "I suppose Mom and Nanny have been at it since the crack of dawn?"

"Of course. You wouldn't believe the lists Mom and I have already been through."

"Yes, I would. What time is it—when did you get here?"

"It's nine now. I've been here an hour. Steven and I drove up from Philadelphia yesterday and stayed with friends in Boston last night. I took the train out this morning."

"Ah." Cassie gets to her feet.

"I had no idea what a madhouse this would be," Penny says anxiously. "I *told* Mom I want a simple wedding. Why does she have to make everything so complicated?"

"You know Mom; she likes to control. Are you all right, Pen?"

"Oh sure, I'm fine," she says. She looks almost manic.

"Excited?"

"Not exactly. I haven't had a chance to get excited. I can't believe we're actually getting married tomorrow. And I really can't believe I'm having a baby!"

"When are you going to tell people—about the baby?" *Why didn't you think to tell me? Your* sister!

"Not till I start looking fat." Penny stands. "Nice haircut, Cassie. Sort of Farrah Fawcett."

"It's a shag. My hair's so curly that with all the layering it gets kind of wild."

"I like it," Penny says. "Well, I should go find Mom. I'll tell her you're up." She grabs Cassie's hand and hugs her.

Cassie turns on the radio and listens to the Beatles sing "I'll Follow the Sun" while she washes her face. After she pulls on a gauzy cotton blouse and shorts, she scrutinizes herself in the mirror. The fabric of the blouse is thin—her bra is visible—but its ruffles are strategically placed, so she looks decent. She hurries through the upper hall. The house is beginning to lose its damp feel; all the windows are open to the hot air.

In the kitchen Penny is skimming the *Boston Globe* as she tells her mother, "I don't care where you put the Roses. Do whatever you want; it's fine with me." She notices Cassie and says, "Cassie, check out this *Doonesbury* cartoon. Mark Slackmeyer is interviewing a jogger, who says, 'A jogger's high is a very pleasant trancelike state the jogger enters after the first half hour of exercise. The lack of oxygen actually makes him hallucinate.'" She glances up. "Hey, what happened to your glasses?"

"I got soft contacts." Cassie puts the kettle on.

Liz says, "There's milk for your tea in the other refrigerator."

"Thanks, Mom. You think of everything."

"No big deal." Then she says, "I'll put them in the Pigeon Inn. That way they can hide whenever they want some peace and quiet." She seems impatient and harried.

"Sounds good, Mom," says Cassie.

Penny says, "My favorite *Doonesbury* cartoon was the one where the little girl says, 'It's a baby woman!'"

"What are you talking about?" Liz responds.

"Mom," Cassie explains, "we don't say 'girls' anymore. Grown females are 'women.' That's the joke."

Liz turns to Penny. "Tell me what you want me to do about those friends of Steven's from California—they have children, don't they? They never RSVP'd."

Eyes down, Penny says curtly, "I'm sure they're coming—assume they are. Is there room for them in the Cottage?"

Cassie notices the love on their mother's face as Liz gazes at Penny, but her sister doesn't. Has their mother ever looked at her that way? Not that she can recall. Penny, the youngest, is their mother's favorite, and it isn't fair. Cassie has always been the good girl—Penny the one who got caught shoplifting a skirt when she was thirteen.

Liz tells Penny, "Your father is picking Martin up at the airport on his way here. What time do you expect Steven?"

From the front of the house a voice calls, "Halloo?"

"Oh, God," says Liz, "who can that be so soon?"

Penny goes to see; Liz lights a cigarette.

"What should I be doing, Mom?"

"Sit down and drink your tea. I'm not ready—"

Penny hurries back. "It's the tent people. I didn't know we were going to have a tent. Tents make me think of country clubs."

"I'll talk to them," Liz says, leaving the kitchen.

"I'm not sure I can stand this," says Penny as soon as Liz is out of earshot. "Things have gotten so elaborate. I *told* Mom I want everything simple. Why did *you* get married, Cassie?"

She's taken aback. No one has ever asked her why she married Martin. "It seemed like the right thing to do. Come on, sit down with me."

Penny joins her at the table.

"What's going to happen with your music?"

"I'm not good enough to make a career out of it."

"Really? I think you're a wonderful flautist."

"I enjoy playing, but I wouldn't want to go on the road, traveling to gigs. Anyway, let's get out of here before Mother comes back. Want to take a walk?"

After a big gulp of tea, Cassie says, "Sure." She grabs her oversized sunglasses.

They move out through the back garden, where their mother is consulting with a man who is saying, "Now whot about onings for this side heah?"

"No, I don't think we need awnings. Just the tent. But I'm glad you talked me into the twenty-by-thirty—I can see now you were right—we really do need the big one." She notices Penny and Cassie. "Where are you two off to?"

Penny says, "We thought we'd take a walk—"

"Don't be long. I want you to put up some signs on the road to help people find their way. When Nanny gets back, she'll need help distributing the breakfast stuff among the houses, but that can all wait a little while. I'll deal with the caterers when they arrive—should be any minute."

"We're off then," says Cassie.

Down the road, Penny asks, "Why do we need signs? We've sent everybody maps showing how to get here. It's not *that* hard to find."

"What if people forget their maps? It can't hurt to make things easier."

"I guess."

"It's simpler to go along with Mom," Cassie says.

"You're right about that."

They pass alongside a stand of bay trees. Penny says, "These shrubs used to be a lot taller, didn't they?"

"You remember them from when we were younger and shorter."

"I suppose."

At the end of the trail they come out upon a huge ledge of pale gray granite. It is a gloriously sunny, still day. As the sisters work their way across the rock, Cassie notices the round foot-wide indentations across its face. "Look," she teases, "dinosaur prints!"

"Nice try, Cassie. You can't fool me with that anymore."

Cassie sits on one of the boulders tumbled near the edge of the water and stares at the horizon. Penny inspects a tide pool, and then she sticks her foot in the water.

Cassie says, "I'm glad you picked Granite Cove for your wedding. It gave me a chance to stop by Smith—"

Wiggling her toes, Penny interrupts. "I sort of had an affair last winter."

Shocked, Cassie says, "What! Why?"

"It didn't mean anything. It was just an experiment."

"Does Steven know about this?"

"No."

Annoyed that Penny would lay this piece of information on her on the eve of her wedding, Cassie says, "You've got to tell him, Penny."

"No, I don't. Anyway, it's none of your business."

Suddenly furious, Cassie exclaims, "You made it my business by telling me!" She walks away to glare at the ocean, trying to calm down. *What am I supposed to do with this information?*

Penny sits down and begins to stir the water in the tide pool with her hands. "Steven and I will have a fine life together. We're good friends; we like the same things. And he's got great genes—deciding who's going to father your children is the one area in life where women have *all* the power. We decide whose genes will survive. I want to make the best possible choice for my children."

Cassie turns back to her sister. "May I say something?"

Penny chuckles. "You can say anything so long as it's about me."

"Are you sure you've chosen the right man?"

"Absolutely."

Sometimes I wonder about my own choice, Cassie thinks. But she won't dwell on that. "I thought you were on the pill, Penny."

"I was, but sometimes I forgot to take it."

Penny courts trouble yet never has to pay a price. "Did you intend to get pregnant?"

"I'm not sorry."

"You're awfully young to be married."

"Yeah, but I know what I want." Rubbing her hands dry on her Bermuda shorts, Penny stands. "It's such a relief to be able to talk about this—I feel better. Thank you."

Feeling unsettled by Penny's disclosure, Cassie says, "I'm going to head up the hill. I won't be long."

"Don't tell anyone, all right, Cassie? Not even Martin."

Now that she's by herself, the timelessness of the place settles over Cassie. Granite Cove had been paradise when she was a child roaming this giant playground of grass and rocks and beach. Today life is much more complicated. Penny has had a fling she plans to keep secret from the man she's about to marry. And, of course, her pregnancy is another secret.

Christopher's family's summer place is up the hill. This is her opportunity to find out if he's there. On the plane east she'd wondered whether she would get to glimpse Christopher this time at Granite Cove. She hasn't laid eyes on him in ages, though she's heard bits of news about him from her mother and grandmother. She and Christopher had been such good friends as children, and then they'd dated until he graduated from Milton Academy. During high school he'd come down from Boston for parties at Norwich Academy, and they'd gone to each other's proms.

Lighting a cigarette, she walks up a steep path. Has her first love changed? At the top of the hill, when she spots a red VW convertible with a black top outside the Bennetts' cottage, she quickly extinguishes her cigarette in the grass and sticks the butt in her pocket. She hurries to the front door. Knocks.

A tall man in a black T-shirt and frayed cut-off jeans opens the door. "Cassie!" He throws his arms around her in a fierce hug that goes on and on.

When he releases her, she says, "Wow!"

He steps back. "Sorry, you caught me by surprise. I'm just so glad to see you after all these years."

"Don't apologize. That was nice."

"Please, come in."

They stand awkwardly, looking at each other. Her heart speeds up.

"What brings you to Granite Cove? It's been eight years since we—"

"Since you broke up with me."

He winces, and she notices the sadness in his dark blue eyes.

"Penny's getting married tomorrow on the lawn at the Rock Lodge. Actually, one time during college I saw you here, but you didn't notice me—you were busy with friends. Your hair was down to your shoulders then."

He reaches a hand toward her but then stops himself and quickly jerks it back to his side. "Can you sit a minute?"

She recalls her to-do list but follows him into the front room, where they take adjacent chairs.

Christopher's auburn hair is darker now. His sideburns extend below his ears, and he's not nearly as svelte as he was in high school. Now he looks like a man. Her nerves start to fizz.

"Penny's getting married?"

"It's kind of sudden," she replies. "You should join us for the festivities this weekend. I'm sure Mom and Dad would love to see you."

"Maybe I will."

His gaze is so intense as he scrutinizes her face.

"You look great, Cassie."

Nonplussed by the closeness of his examination, she says, "Last I heard you were in law school?"

"I passed the bar last summer. I work for the Massachusetts Public Interest Research Group."

"That must be interesting."

"I like it a lot. I get to stay at Granite Cove this summer, and it's an easy commute into Boston by train. I work from here on Fridays."

"You lucky bum. We have so much to catch up on, I hardly know where to start." Glancing down, she sees that his bare feet look almost as familiar as her own. Lifting her eyes, she says, "Going to Berkeley must have been mind-blowing."

"Protesting the Vietnam War was my thing."

"Then you went to Alaska?"

Christopher jumps up from his chair and starts moving around the room. "I worked on a fishing boat off Kodiak Island with an interesting bunch of guys."

That's where he got those shoulders.

"In Alaska, I really learned what a privileged life I've had. I got a job in Anchorage working for an organization that helps native people gain access to the social services they need."

"Good for you." He's talking so fast it's unnerving. "Come back here. I'm not going to bite."

It appears that he has to force himself to sit down again. He digs into his pocket for a cigarette and lights up. After a long exhale, he asks, "How did you like Carleton, Cassie?"

"It was wonderful. Fascinating classmates, excellent professors."

"And then?"

"I worked for a law firm in Minneapolis. I thought that would be interesting, but it turned out to be a job as a glorified secretary taking lots of phone calls, writing letters, arranging meetings for the attorneys."

He says, "You must have been bored out of your mind."

He knows me so well. The realization makes her flush. She crosses her legs and twitches her foot back and forth to dispel her excess energy. "I started thinking about the kinds of work women have typically done—you know, as teachers, nurses, secretaries—and I realized that I have bigger ambitions for myself. I considered going to law school."

"Mother told me you're a graduate student at the University of Minnesota."

"That's right. I'm working on a PhD in women's history."

"What exactly is women's history?"

I still love this man.

Christopher leaps to his feet. "Wait. Can I get you something to drink?"

"No, thanks. I should go soon." But she's grateful for the interruption. "Women's history is a new academic field."

"Women have their own separate history?" He sounds dubious.

"No, women's history is embedded in the past, but traditionally historians only studied men who made names for themselves in war or religion or politics or business."

"Right . . ."

"Well, women were there in all those places too, on battlefields, in churches, organizing campaigns, running shops, flying planes."

"Okay."

"Activities associated with women, like family, and childrearing, and housework, are also worth studying."

"Really? How do you study housework?" He tamps his cigarette out.

"Never mind. I guess my point is that women deserve consideration as more than simply adjuncts or servants to men. It wasn't that long ago that Stokely Carmichael said, 'The only position for women in SNCC is prone.'"

"Ouch."

"Lots of women were involved in the civil rights movement, but they were relegated to sexist roles." In her frustration that women involved in the Student Nonviolent Coordinating Committee had to make the coffee, Cassie taps her cigarette too vigorously against the side of the ashtray. She sprays ashes all over the table. "Oops. Sorry."

"No problem. The cleaning lady comes on Monday." He grins.

"You have a cleaning lady?"

"Just kidding. Socialists don't have cleaning ladies."

"You're a socialist?"

"Are you sure I can't get you something to drink?"

Her stomach feels tense. "Well, maybe if you have a Coke."

He jumps up. "I'll go see what I have in the fridge."

Why does he seem so tightly wound?

When he returns with a glass filled with Coke and ice, he hands it to her.

She takes a sip. "Thank you, Chris. That's good." She sets the drink down. "You said you're a socialist?"

"I believe everyone should have what they need but no more than the essentials."

"Wait a minute! How do you explain your summer cottage? That's not exactly consistent." She chuckles to let him know she's teasing.

"It's not mine; it belongs to my parents. Anyway, this place only has two rooms. It's simple—more like a camp than anything."

"Does being a socialist explain why you're wearing an old T-shirt with a huge hole in it?" She smiles as she leans forward and lightly squeezes his forearm.

"I didn't know you'd be stopping by." He sounds slightly annoyed.

"Just kidding!"

"Sorry, I didn't mean to snap at you. I guess I'm embarrassed you caught me in such grubby clothes."

"That's okay. Anyway, money doesn't really matter all that much to me either, though I know I'm lucky I don't have to worry about having enough. I like being able to buy nice things. Martin's the one who really cares about money. And success, especially success."

"What does he do?"

"He's the son of a small restaurant owner who never went to college. Martin . . ."

Cassie once thought she would marry Christopher, so it feels too weird to talk to him about her husband. She pauses. "What I really want to tell you about is the discovery I made. Yesterday at Smith College I found a collection of diaries belonging to my great aunt, Kate Reed Easton. Actually, she's my great-*grand*aunt. She lived in Paris for a time, and she was involved in the suffrage and birth control movements early in the century. It's so exciting!"

"I've never heard of her. She was a suffragette?"

"Suffragist. The word *suffragette* was used as a put-down."

"I didn't know that."

"Along with the diaries, I saw copies of some suffrage cartoons that were printed in newspapers. She called one 'Meanwhile They Drown.' A man stands on a wharf holding a Votes for Women life preserver. Below him in rough water are women and babies struggling with monsters labeled Sweatshop, Disease, Filth, and White Slavery. The man remarks to a fashionably dressed woman sitting on an anti-suffrage box, 'When ALL women want it, I will throw it to them.' The woman on the box says, 'We don't need it.'"

"Hmmm. That's a little hard to visualize. I guess I've never really thought much about women's issues. For me it's civil rights, native rights."

"Do you still love to play tennis, Chris?"

"I do, but I can't always find someone to play with. These days I'm more likely to go swimming."

They sit in companionable silence for a few moments. Then the song playing on the radio begins to penetrate Cassie's consciousness. "You Can Close Your Eyes." She says, "James Taylor."

"Nice song." Christopher stretches his legs out in front of him.

Cassie says, "I'm still learning who I am and trying to figure out what I want."

"Me too."

"Do you have a special someone in your life?"

"Not really."

"I thought some smart woman would have grabbed you a long time ago."

"I guess I'm easily bored, CayCay. I've learned not to get too serious about anyone."

"Oh." His using her nickname makes her feel as though he just embraced her again. She knows she ought to leave and help her mother, but she really doesn't want to. It's so good to be here with him. Five more minutes . . .

CHAPTER 4

Back at the Bungalow, Nanny tells Cassie, "I made blueberry muffins to go with lunch. Where have you been? You look like you've been running."

"I was just catching up with Christopher. Did you pick the blueberries, Nanny? I thought the season came and went in July."

"I had to buy these. They must come from Maine." Nanny dries her hands. "Christopher still isn't married, I hear."

"You hear correctly."

"Sit down. You can have the first muffin out of the oven. Iced tea, Cassie?"

"Let me get it, Nanny. Would you like some?"

Soon, they are seated together on the Bungalow's tiny porch. Nanny hoists her glass. "To a happy wedding."

"Right," Cassie says. She shifts position on the chaise lounge and sits cross-legged. Nanny stares at her shorts.

"I wish you wouldn't sit that way, Cassie. From this angle, I can see your hairs."

Shocked, Cassie straightens her legs and squeezes them together. Did Christopher get the same view of her crotch?

"There's nothing attractive about hairs," Nanny observes. "Your brother is just as bad. Worse, really. He doesn't wear anything under his shorts, and his balls hang out. I don't want to be forced to look at his balls—they're very unattractive. I've had to speak to him about it more than once. It was so different in my day. When I was a girl, we weren't allowed to sit on the grass in our long dresses. Nice girls didn't sit on the grass." Nanny pulls the hem of her skirt down another couple of inches. "That was simply the way things were done. Ladies *never* wore trousers."

"I've never seen you in pants, Nanny."

"I wear trousers for gardening—it's difficult to be decorous in a skirt when you're down on your hands and knees—but that's the only time I do." Watching the bay, Nanny raises her hand to shade her eyes. "Who's that in the sailboat?"

Cassie looks at the sleek sloop approaching the shore. "I have no idea, Nanny. Too bad Mom's not here. She'd know."

"Liz is a great sailor. At least she used to be." Nanny turns back to Cassie. "I've been thinking you ought to talk to my sister Charlotte. She's an aficionado of history too. She's doing a project on the family—"

"Aunt Charlotte is coming? I can't wait to meet her!"

"You've met her."

"I don't think so."

"I'm sure you met her when you were a baby. Her husband hated it here, so she hasn't visited for . . . oh, decades. But he died a couple of years ago. Now she spends the summers up the hill. She'll be at the wedding."

"That's fantastic. I can ask her about Aunt Kate."

Uncrossing her legs, Nanny leans her elbows on her thighs. "Now tell me what I can do to help your mother. Maybe I should simply stay out of the way. But I want to be useful—"

The timer on the stove dings. "That'll be the muffins," Nanny says. "Take them out and help yourself."

"Do you want one, Nanny?"

"Not right now."

When Cassie returns with a hot blueberry muffin, Nanny is inspecting the signet ring on her little finger. "See how worn this has become? You can hardly tell it's a griffin on a crown." She stretches her right hand out to Cassie.

Cassie puts the muffin down and takes her grandmother's hand. "It *is* getting worn. That must be because the face is rounded. Mine's much squarer." Cassie takes a bite of her muffin. Thinking about Penny's confession, she asks, "Nanny, what does it take to make a happy marriage? After sixty years with Grandpa, you must have a pretty good—"

Nanny speaks over Cassie. "If there are any problems in your marriage, Cassie, I don't want to know about it."

"I wasn't . . ." Actually, Cassie wonders whether her marriage is doomed. Martin's a very traditional, conservative man; he has strong expectations and assumptions about the proper role a wife should play. She once had those same assumptions herself—but not any longer. She asked him to read *The Feminine Mystique* to help him understand the changes in her thinking. He said he didn't have time.

"The trouble with your generation is you think too much about yourselves." Flicking her hand dismissively, Nanny adds, "When your grandfather and I were first married, we spent our evenings canvassing for the Community Chest. If you want to be happy, do for others."

Stung, Cassie says, "I do for others. I try to do more, but with school I don't have much time."

"I'm sorry to hear that. There are people who haven't had our advantages. We have a duty to them."

"Well." Cassie finds it strange to hear her grandmother deliver one of her late grandfather's favorite harangues. And she feels guilty too. "I'll do more for others right now. I'll go back up to the Lodge and see what I can do for Mom."

"A better idea than wasting time with Christopher," replies Nanny.

—

The Lodge is seething with activity. A deliveryman is hauling cartons of liquor and mixes from the back of an Ipswich Liquors truck. In the garden behind the porch, the tent men shout to one another. In the kitchen, Penny is making egg salad sandwiches.

"People have started to arrive, Cassie," she says. "Father and Martin are here; Steven just called from the Esso station for directions."

"Martin's here?"

Liz walks briskly into the room. "I'm going to Nanny's to get our lunch ready. You and Penny hold the fort for a while, okay, Cassie? Oh, and have a talk with your father, if you will."

"Sure, Mom." Ignoring Penny's inquiring glance, she asks, "Where's the list of housing assignments? We should have that available, so we can send people to the right places when they arrive—"

"It's on the table on the porch," Liz says, heading out the door.

"Great minds," Cassie replies.

The phone rings. Penny dashes down the hall to answer it. At the same time a guy in a UPS uniform appears on the front porch, pushing a handcart stacked with boxes. Cassie signs for the delivery, stashes the boxes in a corner, and then looks for her husband. She finds Martin in the living room, his back to the door, inspecting a ceramic medallion mounted on the far wall. Silently she opens the screen door and tiptoes over to touch his shoulder.

He jumps. "You startled me." He appears to be embarrassed that she caught him examining one of the antiques.

"Hi, Martin," she says. He looks rumpled but more handsome than usual.

He kisses her lightly. "I had no idea your family's houses are right on the water. And they have names—you never told me it was like this."

It never occurred to her that it might seem strange to give houses

names. Martin's perspective on things often forces her to reexam-
ine customs she takes for granted. She enjoys that about him. "Let's
get your luggage upstairs. We've been assigned the master bedroom,
which is a treat—I've never slept in that room before. Usually Mom
and Dad take it, but they'll be down at the Bungalow with Nanny
this weekend."

As they head up the main staircase, he asks, "How many bedrooms does this place have?"

"Seven, if you count the sleeping porch at the end of the hall." She
opens the door to their bedroom. "We're lucky; we have our own
bathroom and shower. Here, you take this bureau. My stuff is in the
other one."

He sets down his suitcase and gives her a big hug. "I missed you."

She stands still for several heartbeats. "I missed you too."

Pulling away, he says, "Tell me all." He unpacks while she reports
on her time at Smith and the wedding preparations. She does not
mention Christopher or anything about Penny.

"The documents sound like a treasure trove. You should go back to
Smith and see what else they have."

"We'll see," she replies neutrally. It irritates her when he instructs
her on how to handle her own work. "Tell me what you've been doing
since I left."

He recounts meetings and conversations at the office and an invitation to a party that came in the mail. "Oh, I scheduled a date to play
bridge with Dan and Linda next weekend."

"Are you ready for your trial on Monday?"

"Pretty much."

"What about Lucy? Was she unhappy about going to Camp
Canine?"

"Cassie, dogs don't have feelings. They simply operate on instinct.
You have way too active an imagination when it comes to Lucy and
her putative thoughts and feelings."

They've had this argument before. Cassie believes imagination enables her to empathize with the experiences of others. It's what helps to bring history alive for her.

"Tell me, how did Dad seem on your drive from the airport?"

"As usual, he plied me with questions, so I did most of the talking."

"Mother's been worried about him."

"He seems fine to me, Cassie." He smiles at her. "I need to stretch my legs. Want to show me around the property?"

"I should stay here to welcome people."

"I'll take a look on my own then."

After he leaves, she sits on the bed to read just a little more of Kate's diaries.

April 16, 1914: A brisk breeze and heavy torrents of rain during the night have washed away all the gray remnants of winter, and today the world appears brand-new, all clean and brilliant with color and light. Now the grass is greener, the tree trunks a darker umber than yesterday; even the sky seems a deeper blue.

The air is so fresh and exhilarating that I feel I could do anything today. Truly what I want is to make some lasting contribution to mankind—the little acts of charity which I perform for the needy simply do not answer my deep desire to be of service. What might this contribution be? There has to be some way in which I could help enable impoverished young women to attend college and improve the likelihood of their employment in a responsible position. This would require underwriting the tuition and living expenses for a few worthy women; I wonder what the expenses are these days for one woman to attend Smith, Radcliffe, or Bryn Mawr for four years? And how would I find the most talented and diligent? How could I make the availability of such assistance known to those who might need it? These thoughts are rousing my brain.

<u>January 3, 1915</u>: Del is very pleased; he has been invited to prepare the fern section of the seventh edition of *Gray's Manual of Botany,* and while I am happy for him, I must admit here that I envy him a little. I wish that I had something like that, some work of my own that consumed me as much as his does him. His mind is so filled with his discoveries that he frequently leaves the table before Mrs. Easton and I have even finished eating.

<u>February 16, 1915</u>: Despite the objections of Del's mother, I marched in a suffrage parade today, and it was absolutely thrilling! Organized by the Massachusetts Woman Suffrage Association and local Equal Suffrage leagues, the parade celebrated passage at the State House of the Mondell Resolution, which asked for a Constitutional amendment eliminating "male" from the qualification to vote. A marching band accompanied the parade all the way to suffrage headquarters in Boston.

While I have always believed fervently in suffrage for women, the experience of marching in the ranks with other suffragists gave me a sense of participation in something really big, and now my soul is afire with the vision of all that this great movement can accomplish.

Perhaps I shall even be able to change Mrs. Easton's thinking once I become armed with more information about the difference woman suffrage will make for us all.

<u>March 10, 1915</u>: Bearing the torch first ignited by Susan B. Anthony and others many decades ago, undeterred by the

defeats of the past, we are driving toward *complete* equality for women now. Suffrage is the key to all our reforms; without it, there is precious little we can do about the dangerous conditions under which many women and children must work, the appalling state of our streets and hospitals (where filth and disease ride rampant), or the recent plague of political corruption.

Once women win the vote, we shall make our voices heard in the Congress and in state houses across the land. Ours is the standard of Progress. Moreover, women shall finally achieve full stature as sentient human beings—no more shall we have to suffer the mortification of being classed under the law with criminals and imbeciles. This is truly a momentous time.

The movement is acquiring momentum as hosts of women come together to better humanity and advance the cause of civilization for the entire race. We cannot fail, for we are indomitable!

I feel so alive now. My old happy confidence has returned, and I know that we shall succeed, however formidable the obstacles. Our immediate task is to reach a majority of the state's voters for the referendum in November.

Classed with criminals and imbeciles! Outrageous. Cassie begins to read the next entry, then hears the sounds of guests arriving. Dutifully, she puts the pages away. Out on the lawn, Penny is greeting some people Cassie doesn't know. She spots her father hovering on the periphery of the group surrounding Penny.

"Cassie!" His tie loose, her father appears rumpled but comfortable. They hug, and she takes his arm, walks him down a path that leads to the beach. The heat feels oppressive now, pierced only by the caws of seagulls.

"Thanks for picking Martin up at the airport."

"It was good to get some time with him. He has a very challenging case in front of him."

"So I've heard. How did your drive up from Connecticut go, Dad?"

"I treated myself to fried clams at a Howard Johnson's along the way."

"Yum! I bet you had some ice cream too—I know about you and ice cream."

"Actually, I didn't have room for dessert."

"How are things going for you these days, Dad? It's been such a long time since we really talked."

"Well, you know the board hired a new minister, Jeremy Fisher, who's just out of Yale Divinity School. He's still wet behind the ears, but people like talking to him. Counseling members was my favorite part of the job."

"People will always come to talk with you, Dad."

"The younger members of our congregation have started going to him."

"Does this mean you don't have to work quite so hard?"

"My load is a little lighter," he concedes. "And Jeremy preaches once a month, so I don't have as many sermons to prepare."

"That must be a relief."

"I don't feel as needed as I used to," her father admits. "My fear is that the board wants to get rid of me. Hiring Jeremy could be the first step in replacing me."

Cassie stops walking. "Your congregation loves you!"

"I hope so. You're a good daughter, Cassie. I've been feeling somewhat sidelined, but I'm fine. Of course, losing my younger daughter isn't much fun."

"You aren't losing Penny. Soon she'll be giving you a grandchild. You and mom will enjoy that, won't you?"

"Absolutely! Children are God's greatest gift to mankind. I'm thrilled by the prospect of becoming a grandfather."

"I'm glad to hear that, Dad."

"Now, I'm not exactly delighted that Penny got pregnant in advance of marriage, but I know very well that these things happen."

"Do you wish I'd give you a grandchild?"

"No. I understand you have other priorities right now. You get to choose when you're ready to have a baby."

"Thank goodness for birth control! So, tell me, what other news is there about goings on at Norwich Congregational?"

"Your mother's working her fanny off getting the soup kitchen up and running."

"A soup kitchen?"

"At the church. The board went through a planning process to determine our goals for the next five years. We want to move out into the neighborhood and start meeting some of their needs. The soup kitchen is the first step. When your mother heard about that, she volunteered to take it on."

"I bet it suits her a lot better than presiding over the ladies' auxiliary. She doesn't have a lot of patience for schmoozing with chatty women."

"It's a great fit for Liz's talents. She's so immersed that I hardly see her anymore. I have to go to the kitchen whenever I want to talk to her. I can tell I get in the way sometimes."

Coming from the other direction, someone who looks vaguely familiar to Cassie stops when he reaches them. "Paul!" he says to her father. "Good to see you."

"George," her father says, as they shake hands, "you remember my daughter Cassie."

"All grown up now," George replies. "I'm glad we ran into each other, Paul. There's something I'd like to discuss with you."

"I'll leave you to it," Cassie says. She turns back toward the Lodge.

The phone is ringing; presents are gathered on the table. Steven stands in the middle of the porch with his arm around Penny.

"There you are, Cassie," Steven says. A large man, he grabs her and gives her a bear hug. "Isn't this exciting, sister-in-law-to-be?"

She's a little surprised by the hug. She only met Steven last Christmas, but she has to grin at his exuberance. "Yes, it is."

He says, "I know you've been helping a lot. We've got everything under control now, so you can relax."

"Great. So, what were you doing in Boston last night?"

"Actually, a friend of mine got us tickets to the Red Sox game."

"Cool." She doesn't know what else to say to him. "Have you seen Martin?"

"He's wandering around somewhere."

The phone rings. Cassie excuses herself and goes to answer it. The caller asks for directions from the rotary at the end of Route 128. The phone keeps ringing, and arriving delivery people keep Cassie busy. After another hour of this, she climbs the stairs back to the bedroom, where the diaries await.

April 1, 1915: Virginia Wiley arrived from the national office of the American Woman Suffrage Association to guide our efforts in the state association over the next six months. Then she plans to move on to the campaign in the West.

Although Virginia's prim attire might lead one to assume that she is timid, the moment she speaks one is struck by the intensity of her emotions. As an organizer, she is truly inspiring. She has managed to shape our disparate group of women from all ranks of society into a dynamic, organic whole—finally we are functioning with real efficiency.

Virginia chose me to serve as her personal assistant, and I am thrilled, for I am certain to learn a great deal from her.

Her assurance is contagious. Initially I viewed Virginia's enthusiasm with some mistrust, but I have come to see that she follows her ideas with immediate actions. Moreover, she does not insist that everything be done according to her lights. She leaves much to our own discretion, for she believes in our abilities, and as a result, we are growing sure of ourselves.

<u>April 4, 1915:</u> During a meeting yesterday, while Virginia enumerated several alternatives she is considering for launching the campaign to attract publicity to our cause, I was taken by the thought that a male leader might not have proceeded thus; would he expose the workings of his mind to us as Virginia did? I don't know whether this is a new form of leadership or merely a matter of individual style. Virginia could have informed us of the decision she had already reached, but instead she sought our opinions and she listened carefully before she raised objections to those ideas that hadn't been thoroughly thought through.

It will be fascinating to observe whether she chooses a plan that incorporates some of our . . .

A knock on the door brings Cassie back to the present. It's Penny. "Come down to my room, Cassie. I want to show you something." Cassie files away the pages she's reading and checks the clock: it's almost five already. *I'm supposed to jump whenever Penny calls?*

As she walks down the hall, the house seems expectant with a pre-party hush. When Cassie looks into Penny's room, her sister is brushing her long hair. "What do you think?" she asks, turning from the mirror. "Will I pass muster with Nanny?"

Cassie takes in her long-sleeved cream blouse and cotton skirt, which is striped with wide sections of gray and narrow bands of rose. Penny's face glows.

"You look lovely, Penny. The skirt and blouse are perfect. But you're not wearing a bra."

"I'm so flat I don't need to."

Cassie wonders whether that will change as Penny's pregnancy progresses.

Penny picks up a black velvet jeweler's box and hands it to Cassie. "How about these earrings? Steven gave them to me before he went to the Inn to change. I think it would be good if I wore them, but do they go with this getup?"

"Put them on."

Penny takes off her gold hoops and inserts the pearl studs. "Well?"

"They're gorgeous."

Turning her head from side to side in the mirror, Penny says, "They are pretty, aren't they? I was totally surprised. Steven is so generous."

Cassie sits on the bed. "You look happy."

"I am." Penny perches next to Cassie and looks into her eyes. "My fling had nothing to do with Steven and me and *our* relationship. It helped me become certain that I want to marry Steven."

"I hope you know what you're doing."

"Don't worry, Cassie. You should get changed, too. I can see you *are* wearing a bra."

Cassie hurries back down the hall and finds Martin in their room, flopped on the bed. "Martin? The bridal dinner starts at six."

"All right." He rises reluctantly.

She knows he doesn't want to be here. They had a huge fight when she learned about the wedding and informed him that they must attend. She told him, "Attendance is not optional for family weddings and funerals."

He said, "I've got a very tough trial starting on the Monday after that weekend. It's not the least bit convenient for me to come east. I'd much rather stay home preparing my case."

"I know, Martin, and I'm sorry the timing works out like this, but it's my only sister's *wedding*. You can't skip it."

"If you really insist, I guess I have to come."

"Thank you."

"I must admit, I've been wondering when I'd ever get an invitation to visit Granite Cove."

"Why didn't you say so? I thought you preferred spending vacation time in northern Minnesota."

"You never suggested we go to Granite Cove."

"You never asked."

"Well, at least I'll get to spend some time with Paul."

Remembering this conversation, Cassie is grateful that at least Martin likes her father. She suspects he's intimidated by her mother and that he considers Penny a lightweight.

Now Martin asks, "What's the dress code tonight?"

"I told you to bring a suit, but actually a jacket and tie would be better."

"I brought both."

"I knew you would—you like to be prepared."

CHAPTER 5

Guests circle around Steven and Penny on the porch, others stand in groups on the front lawn, and a teenaged server weaves through with a plate of hot cheese puffs. Another appears with water chestnuts wrapped in bacon. Cassie joins her mother and grandmother.

"Don't you look nice, Cassie!"

Cassie has donned an Indian print caftan that hides her thick Scottish legs and ankles. And her favorite sandals, bought years ago in Greenwich Village when she fancied herself a hippie.

Liz continues, "Is that a new dress? It's the same blue as your eyes. Very becoming."

"Thanks, Mom. I like what you're wearing too. That shade of lavender is definitely your color."

"The lawn furniture looks crummy—we should have painted it."

"It's fine. Don't worry about it, Mom."

"You look very nice," Nanny states. "As does Penny. Though I hope tomorrow she'll wear her hair up." Nanny calls out, "You have such a lovely neck, Penny, I'd like to be able to see it."

It's clear from Penny's expression that she's never before considered how her neck looks. She turns back to Steven.

"Where *are* Steven's parents, the Roses?" Nanny asks Liz. "I want to meet them."

"I met them when they arrived," says Liz.

Nanny remarks, "It's beyond belief that I would never have met the parents of the man my granddaughter is marrying. In my day—"

"There wasn't time, Nanny."

"Times sure have changed, Cassie, and I can't say it's for the better."

"Here, let's get Penny to introduce us," says Cassie. "I haven't met them either."

As they move through the crowd, Nanny takes Cassie's hand in a rare gesture of affection. A moment later, when they join the couple who must be the Roses, she lets go.

Estelle Rose appears nervous; her jaunty gypsy dress suits her deep tan and dark hair. Next to her, Lester Rose radiates pride. After introductions and the obligatory remarks on the happiness of the event, Estelle says, "This house is beautiful. I like the windows and the door out to the garden in back. Makes a lovely breezeway."

Nanny says, "I'm glad we can close that door when it's windy. Sometimes the garden in back is the only place you can get warm. The house is unique, isn't it? My mother designed it."

"Is that right?"

"She hired an architect, but he said her ideas wouldn't work, so she got rid of him and found a contractor who'd do what she wanted."

"She must have been quite a woman." Estelle sounds awed and a little wary. "It's such an unusual location for a wedding. My friends' children usually have their parties at the country club."

Penny says, "We wanted something less formal."

"The porch was the main point of contention. The architect said it would never work to have such a big open expanse the whole width of the house with no supports beyond the walls, especially with rooms above. Mother insisted granite block walls and concrete floors could bear the weight. And she was right. This place has weathered every storm and hurricane since 1911."

"Sure looks sturdy to me," says Les.

Cassie points out Aunt Grace, Uncle Rick, and Martin chatting together. Estelle asks about a knot of people in the midst of an uproarious reunion on the grass—Penny explains they're classmates of Steven's from Jefferson Medical School.

Penny calls Estelle's and Les's attention to her father, who is moving among clusters of people, stopping here and there to chat, while Liz floats alongside him like a queen. When Penny takes her soon-to-be in-laws over to speak with her parents, Cassie decides it is time for a drink.

The young man standing behind the bar has long curly brown hair; he looks just like one of the Bee Gees.

"What can I get for you, ma'am?"

"I'd like a tonic water on ice with lime."   ,

He turns his back to prepare her drink and then offers her a tall glass, saying, "Nice view you have here."

"Thank you. We're very lucky."

Penny interrupts, "Excuse me. Look who's here, Cassie!" A large woman stands nearby hanging onto the hand of a little boy who is trying to hide behind her. *Now what does Penny want from me?* "It's Gabrielle, the artist I told you about. She and Norman and their son just arrived all the way from San Francisco!"

"Clearly Penny's sister," Gabrielle says. "I'm glad to meet you."

"Welcome," says Cassie.

"Cassie, would you show Gabrielle down to the Cottage? Norman and Steven are busy with their med school buddies, and I should stick around."

"Of course, Penny." She envies her sister's ability to ask directly for what she wants—though it feels like Penny takes her for granted.

As they head to the Cottage, Cassie says, "You're a painter?"

Gabrielle stops and leans over to hear her son's whisper. As her long wheat-colored hair hides both their faces, she looks like some sort of earth mother. Is that what Penny admires about her? Then

Gabrielle straightens up. "Until we moved this summer, I was working on a series of women, my great-grandmother and her sisters, all immigrants from Norway. We've almost finished settling into our new home, and I really look forward to getting back to my painting this fall."

"Painting your ancestors sounds fascinating. Are you working from photographs?"

"I am. The faces are so real—expressive and strong. Everything they experienced in their lives is reflected. My challenge is to depict that strength without making them look wooden. It's my version of *Roots*."

"I watched that miniseries. Wasn't it great? It seemed like everyone I knew was watching it at the same time. *Roots* really resonated for me."

"How so?"

"It's time people who have been invisible to history get 'discovered.' I just completed my master's thesis on women who organized themselves into clubs and hospital auxiliaries in the nineteenth century. I love how revolutionary they were. Have you shown any of your work?"

"I'd like to," Gabrielle admits. "I might talk to some galleries once I finish this series. I think the paintings have a value beyond the personal; everybody has a history."

Cassie touches Gabrielle's arm. "I agree!"

Gabrielle says, "Learning about your ancestors is important if you want to know yourself. The more you understand where you came from and the challenges and difficulties your predecessors survived, the more you'll find to take pride in. We all need that."

"It *is* inspiring to find a role model in one of your ancestors. I just discovered one myself—Aunt Kate. She was a painter. And she drew suffrage cartoons. An independent woman in my own family."

Gabrielle looks into Cassie's eyes. "That's wonderful. Now you know you don't have to live your mother's life."

Cassie feels as though she's suddenly been liberated. "You're right, Gabrielle. Thank you!"

They arrive at the Cottage and get Gabrielle and her son settled. After a few moments Cassie says, "I should go back to the party now. Are you going to stay down here?"

"Yes. I want to make sure Luke sleeps."

"I'd be glad to bring you some dinner if you'd like."

"No, thanks, Cassie. I brought some things for Luke—he's a little fussy. Go join your sister and her guests. I hope we can talk again later."

"We have the whole weekend ahead of us. See you soon."

Walking along the road back to the Lodge, Cassie listens to a host of crickets, their song punctuated by the voice of a bullfrog from the lily pond. Could the reason she's often so impatient with her mother be that she has unconsciously assumed she has to be as restricted in her life options as her mother has been?

Now people are sitting all over the porch and lawn, eating steamed clams. On her way to the kitchen for clams of her own, Cassie thinks about what she might do when she gets back to Minnesota. Maybe she should volunteer with the National Organization for Women or the local chapter of Planned Parenthood? It's her own life. She should do what she wants with it.

Then she walks by her mother and her mother's brother, Uncle John, deputy director of the U.S. Environmental Protection Agency.

"What's the story on red tide?" Liz asks, as she dips a clam into a cup of broth and then into butter.

Uncle John replies, "It's a relatively recent phenomenon. We don't have evidence of red tides fifty years ago."

"Is it caused by all the garbage that gets dumped in the ocean?" Liz drops a clam into her mouth.

"We don't know for sure. But it's definitely becoming worse with pollution. Some clam diggers have been forced out of business by red . . ."

As she continues to move through the crowd, it occurs to Cassie that her mother is better informed than Cassie expects. Then she passes the groom's mother and Nanny leaning toward each other above the plates on their laps. Over in the corner she sees her father engrossed in a tête-à-tête with a tall man she doesn't recognize. Her father keeps nodding his head encouragingly. Cassie walks by the groom, and he says, "Hey, Cassie, come here a minute! I have to talk with you."

Steven is barrel-chested and has a deep, gruff voice, but his eyes are exceedingly gentle. "I want to thank you. This weekend wouldn't be half as perfect if it weren't for you and all the work you and your mother have done." He kisses Cassie lightly on the forehead and squeezes her hand. *Why doesn't Penny ever thank me?*

"You're welcome, Steven. I hope tomorrow will be the happiest day of your lives."

He says, "We're very grateful."

When she finally has a loaded plate in hand, she looks around for a place to eat.

Aunt Grace pats the empty spot on the sofa next to her. "Sit down, dearie."

Her husband, Uncle Rick, sporting a yellow jacket and madras slacks, says, "Yes, sit down, sit down. Great party. Your ma's outdone herself."

Grace winks at Cassie, and she reminds Cassie of Grandpa; she has never noticed the resemblance before. Leaning around his wife, Uncle Rick says, "What's the latest on the women's lip movement, Cassie? I count on you to keep me up to date."

Grace raises her eyebrows at Cassie, as if to say, *Here he goes again.*

"Women's *lip*? It's women's *liberation*. The movement is about equal treatment—"

"Cassie, you know women aren't equal to men—I've told you before. Women are superior. Ever since Governor Dummer went coed, I've watched the girls in my classes outshine the boys by a mile."

"Girls mature earlier than boys, Uncle Rick."

"That's not it. Girls are stronger and smarter—and they live longer. Men need women to take care of them."

"Women have their own lives to lead."

"Leave men in the dust and then where will you be? What I really don't like is not being able to sing 'hymns' anymore—now we have to sing 'persons.' Right, Cassie?"

"Rick is passionate about his opinions," Grace remarks wryly. Cassie can't tell whether Aunt Grace agrees with Uncle Rick or not. She stands. "I see my husband. If you'll excuse me." She moves to join Martin on the grass. "Uncle Rick is in fine form," she says.

"You know he likes to get your goat, Cassie. He loves to argue. You should give it right back to him. Or start agreeing with him. If you do that, he'll switch positions just to keep you going."

"I suppose," says Cassie.

"Where have you been, anyway? I almost think you've been avoiding me."

She feels a little guilty because she *has* been avoiding him. "Between Mom's orders and Penny's requests, I've been busy." Sinking down on the grass, she says, "Steven said you've been wandering around. So, what do you think of Granite Cove?"

"It's got a certain old-fashioned charm. It reminds me a little of the north shore of Lake Superior, except that the rocks are grayer here and the houses are Cape Cod saltboxes, not dark brown cabins."

"How do you know about saltboxes?" she teases.

"Before I decided on law school, I considered becoming an architect, but then I decided that's much too precarious a profession for a man who wants a family and a nice house." He stretches out his legs, looking more comfortable now that she's paying attention to him.

"I never knew that," she admits.

"You don't know everything about me, sweetie."

She notices the horizon, fiery streaks of red, salmon, and gold arching across the whole sky. "A classic Granite Cove sunset."

"Gorgeous," he replies.

Paul clicks his knife against his glass and calls out to the crowd. "Attention, everyone. I'd like to propose a toast." He raises his arm. "To the Roses. Welcome to the family. We're delighted you're joining us."

"To the Roses" echoes around the yard.

An immensely pregnant woman appears at the edge of the lawn.

Cassie jumps up, crying, "Helen! I've been looking for you."

Martin says, "Remind me who she is."

Pausing briefly, Cassie explains, "She's the cousin I spent the summer after high school with traveling around Europe on Eurail passes. She's also an assistant vice president at the Bank of Boston."

"That's right. She came to our wedding."

Cassie rushes across the lawn to throw her arms around Helen. "May I touch?" she asks.

"Sure." Helen chuckles. "I can't believe how many people want to pat my stomach these days—my body isn't my own private property any longer. Even your father wanted to touch 'the lump.' That's what Frank and I call it."

Gently putting her hand on Helen's belly, Cassie says, "I didn't realize it would feel so solid. Do you want to sit down somewhere?"

The two women retreat to the rocks to watch night descend over the water. "What's it like, being pregnant?" Cassie asks. "Is it awful?"

"No, it isn't. I'm lucky, I haven't felt sick too often. But I'm incredibly tired all the time." Helen extends her legs out in front of her. "I hate having no energy. I want my body back to myself. But I'm trying to go with the flow. It's not easy."

"You look great, all pink and glowing." It occurs to Cassie that

Penny looks the same way. She's aching to confide in Helen about Penny's pregnancy and cheating on Steven. Maybe later. Cassie leans back on her elbows. "What do you like about your current condition?"

"Interesting question," says Helen. "No one's asked me that. I think what I like most is the companionship; this little being is always with me. And I've been learning from this experience—lessons I suspect I'll need once the baby's here—about patience and waiting, not pushing. I've had to slow down."

"How's work?"

"Fine. I'm pretty distracted, but so far, I haven't made any gross errors. Sometimes it's weird being a banker who's pregnant."

"Say more," Cassie says, lighting a cigarette.

"Mmm, that looks good."

"Want one?"

"I quit when I got pregnant."

"Good for you! I'm impressed." Cassie exhales out the side of her mouth so she won't inundate Helen with smoke. "What's strange about being a pregnant banker?"

"It just seems incongruous—pregnancy doesn't fit with my image of being a professional. Don't get me wrong. I love my job."

Thinking about what Gabrielle said earlier, Cassie offers, "Our mothers didn't work—we don't have any role models in our family of working mothers."

"True," Helen agrees. "It really hit me last week. I was on my way to the obstetrician for my monthly checkup, urine sample tucked discreetly into my briefcase, but first I had an appointment with the lawyers for the bank. It was broiling hot, and I was dressed to the nines for the meeting, wearing a silk dress and blazer, high heels, the whole getup. So, there I am standing at the reception desk of the stuffiest law firm in Boston when all of a sudden, I feel this icy drip, drip, drip on my foot."

"Oh no," says Cassie.

"The urine jar was leaking, and it was cold because I'd refrigerated my pee to keep it fresh, and . . ." Helen can't continue, she's laughing so hard.

"I can just see you," Cassie says. "What happened then?"

"I mopped up the mess and went to my meeting. Fortunately, the papers in my briefcase were in a file folder, which ended up protecting them from getting wet."

Cassie and Helen snort and laugh until their stomachs hurt. Finally, wiping her eyes, Cassie says, "Are you going back to work after the baby's born?"

"I assume so. I'll have three months of maternity leave, and then I expect to return to the bank."

"Sounds good."

"Of course," Helen goes on, "I won't really know how I feel until the time comes. Maybe I won't be able to stand leaving the baby with someone else? On the other hand, we can't afford for me to stay home forever."

"Where is Frank?"

"He's gone mountain climbing with some buddies. He figured he'd better take advantage of his freedom while he's still got it. And I'm glad to have a few days to myself."

"A little time alone must be a real treat."

"That's for sure."

"One of Penny's friends told me I don't have to live my mother's life, and the way she put it really hit me. I think part of me has been assuming I'd end up with a life that looks like Mom's, and another part has been struggling to get free of all those expectations, so I can discover my own path."

"I know what you mean," Helen replies. "The real test for me will come after my maternity leave expires. Then what will I do? I don't know."

"Well, I'm really happy you're launching the next generation, Helen."

"But tell me about you, Cassie. How are you coming along with grad school?"

"I found the most amazing stuff at Smith a couple days ago—diaries of my great-grandaunt Kate Reed Easton, who started the Birth Control League here in Massachusetts in 1916. I'm thinking I might be able to do something with this for my dissertation."

"That sounds intriguing."

"I'm really excited. I'll need to go back to Smith to see what else they have."

"Let me know when you come back to Boston. You could stay with us."

"Thanks, Helen. I appreciate the offer."

Helen yawns and then awkwardly gets to her feet. "Remind me—what time is the wedding tomorrow?"

"Three thirty."

"See you then," Helen replies.

Cassie makes her way back to Martin, who stands glowering, his hands on his hips.

"Where the hell have you been?" he says. He sounds furious. "I couldn't find you anywhere."

"Why are you so possessive, Martin? It's like you don't trust me."

"Where were you?"

"Helen and I went over to watch the sunset for a while—"

"I don't have anything to do. All Steven's buddies want to talk about is the doctor business, which doesn't leave me with much to say."

"There's Nanny or Mom or Dad or Penny or—"

"They're busy with people I've never met before."

"Well, I'm sorry if you felt I abandoned you."

They move toward the porch, which is quite dark. The lantern hanging from the center of the ceiling is the only illumination. A few people are scattered around, speaking quietly.

A match flares nearby. "Come on over, Cassie, Martin. We're checking out the stars."

They join Steven on the grass. He says, "It's amazing how bright the stars are out here. You can't even see them in the city."

Martin asks, "Have you always lived in Philadelphia, Steven?"

"My whole life. Where did you grow up, Martin?"

"The Iron Range in northern Minnesota."

"Tomorrow we'll become brothers-in-law. What do you like to do for fun?"

"I love to play tennis."

"Me too! I have rackets in the car."

"I saw a tennis court up the hill while exploring this afternoon."

"Groovy!"

A large boat passing the bell buoy out in the bay causes it to rock, and its tolling sounds mournful to Cassie; she realizes she feels sick to her stomach. "I've got to hang it up, guys."

"Are you all right?" Steven asks.

Maybe she's feeling guilty, or else she's on the verge of getting her period. "I'm tired and I've been smoking too much. G'night."

"Martin, tell me about your work," says Steven.

They continue talking while Cassie leaves them.

Upstairs, she reminds herself to be careful removing her contacts—she can't afford to lose or tear one; she doesn't have any extras. After she puts them in their storage case, she places the case in the little box for heat disinfection, turns it on, and completes the rest of her evening ablutions.

Once she is lying on the bed, her brain begins to spin. *You don't have to live your mother's life. You* don't *have to live your mother's life.* The curtains flutter in a sudden bit of breeze. She is too keyed up to sleep. She turns the light back on and reaches for some pages from Kate's diaries.

April 20, 1915: The Suffrage Association is starting to dis-
integrate into factions: a couple of women have attempted
to dominate the group; some want only to work under
Virginia's wing in order to capture some of her limelight;
and others are squabbling over differences of opinion or
personality.

Despite our common goal, everyone diverges when it
comes to determining the most effective methods for ensuring that we reach all the voters. I think we should employ
stronger tactics of the sort that Carrie Chapman Catt uses
with such great success elsewhere, but Virginia looks on her
as an upstart, even though we are fighting the same battle. I
believe we could learn from Catt.

Nevertheless, this is not the appropriate time for squabbling. To succeed, we must work together as sisters in our
common cause.

The subtle changes that disturb the atmosphere alarm me,
but I seem to be the only one who is troubled. Knowing that
Virginia will not remain with us for long, I balk at worrying her, and besides, I believe the local association officers
need to shoulder more and more of the work. Ordinarily I
ignore the discomforts I perceive around me when I believe
them to be none of my concern, and I do not attend to petty
bickering, but now I must because I believe that if the association does not adopt more dispassionate, modern methods
of organization, we shall lose everything we would win for
women.

I feel certain that we must become less emotional in our
work, and yet I can also see that emotion is the fuel that fires
great enthusiasm and unbounded energies for all we must
undertake.

<u>May 1, 1915:</u> Exhilarated by the work we have accomplished these past weeks, I am devoting most of my time to suffrage now. We developed a wonderfully detailed, coherent set of plans, and soon we shall set them into operation with a variety of activities over the next few months.

This morning Virginia, who is constantly tossing off ideas, had a true inspiration; she said we should find an artist to draw political cartoons about suffrage for the newspapers so that we can appeal to a larger audience and raise wide popular support for the campaign. I am greatly intrigued by the thought. I would like to try. I can certainly draw, though it's been years since I worked at it.

Having neither model nor subject, I am unsure of how to start; I suppose I must imagine a model. Virginia's Amazonian strength of will brings heroic images to mind. Now, where have I buried my sketchbook?

<u>May 10, 1915:</u> The fog surrounding the house presses down upon my spirits; thoughts are as elusive and formless as the thick mist, but this is most inopportune because I have a great deal of work to accomplish.

My task—to write up a complete list of every step we must take, using proper publicity methods, to attract public notice of next month's parade in Springfield—is one which I quail at, for I lack sufficient information to do it thoroughly, but we have already discussed the obstacles at great length; the time for concerted action is approaching.

Today I almost wish I had a lesser position in the association—decision-making can be burdensome. I imagine that it would be easier simply to serve as one of the followers, but then I would miss the satisfaction of helping to determine the course.

Meanwhile, I have not been able to come up with a good cartoon, though I have been trying for days.

Mrs. Easton is in the process of redecorating the front drawing room, and she comes in to interrupt me constantly, seeking my opinion on samples of fabric and paint although she doesn't really care what I think—she simply wants someone to confirm her ideas. Del cannot be bothered with this, so it falls to me to hear her out.

<u>May 11, 1915:</u> Fury has me by the throat: I am nearly choking on my feelings of rage and outrage—how could she treat me so?

Following Virginia's lead, I took the initiative on a few small organizational decisions, and she ridiculed my efforts—she belittled me! Although she conveyed her scorn privately in the sanctum of her office, I believe that was less a matter of policy than of self-protection. I feel certain that had she opened the business up at the weekly meeting, many of the others would have agreed with me.

There is *no need* for her to ridicule me: I have been her staunchest supporter, her best worker. I will never again place myself in a position where Virginia can refuse my suggestions with such heedless cruelty; I shall look no further than my nose since that is what she seems to want. Virginia says that the best is accomplished when each individual attends to her own tasks while one person—Virginia, of course—stands at the center, overseeing the entire operation. She claims that no one else need concern herself with the whole. It appears that she would have me hide my growing competency as an organizer under a barrel.

I am bitterly disappointed—I had hoped that women could forge a new method of leadership, and I believed that

Virginia had done so. I thought that the new woman could participate equally in both the burden and the joy of the work. Must the commander act in an autocratic manner for the mission to succeed?

CHAPTER 6

A chorus of red-winged blackbirds wakes Cassie to another hot day. She carefully extricates herself from the sheets so she won't wake Martin. As soon as her feet reach the concrete floor and she stands, she feels so queasy that she sits down again. The heat is getting to her. After she regains her equilibrium, Cassie checks to see whether she has gotten her period. Not yet. Then she inserts her contacts, showers, and dresses.

The Lodge is quiet as Cassie walks through the upper hall. Downstairs, she finds her mother pacing the empty porch. Liz looks tired but so familiar and dear that Cassie wants to touch her.

"What a nice party that was," she says, kissing her mother on the cheek.

"I've got a long list of wedding-day chores, Cassie. Let's get cracking."

"As soon as I have some tea, Mom."

Sighing, Liz sits down on one of the wicker chairs and takes out her cigarettes. When Cassie returns with her mug of Irish Breakfast, she asks, "Where's Penny? She wasn't in her room when I went by. I expected to see her down here."

"Penny's gone up the hill to wake Steven, though it's a little late for them to sleep separately—closing the barn door after the horse has gone. Anyway, first thing, look in the sheds for some white latex paint—we're going to paint this furniture—it's simply too shabby."

"*Today?*" Cassie's really annoyed. "Fine." She'll go along with her mother for now.

"Find paint, or buy a can, and get someone to do it right away so it'll be dry in time. In this heat the paint won't be wet for long. Then get someone to hose down this porch and wipe the tables. It smells like a dive in here."

"It does smell—the air's so still and muggy. What else?"

"Someone needs to pick up the keg—it's been ordered—and a lot more ice. That job should probably wait until the last minute. Oh, and take all the garbage out to the dumpster. And see what you can do with the flowers. They're drooping." Abruptly she stands and strides out into the sun, where she scans the sky.

Cassie lights a cigarette, leans back in her chair, and stares at the concrete ceiling. She's never noticed all the cracks before. Why does she keep being ordered around and taken for granted when she's doing everything right, whereas everyone goes along with her sister, who cheats, who's in a shotgun wedding, who hogs all the attention? It's not fair. She could cry from frustration and hurt. What does she have to do for her mother to treat her with respect?

Back on the porch a moment later, Liz says, "No sign of rain. Let's move the presents into the living room. We won't need to seat people in there. I'll give you a hand."

While they carry pretty packages wrapped in white and silver to a far corner of the living room, Liz wonders aloud whether they should move the bar out from under the tent. She tells Cassie to think about it. Then she says: "Grace will need help setting things up for lunch. Oh, in the Cottage kitchen you'll find a new plastic garbage can which should be big enough for the keg and ice."

Then Cassie goes up to her bedroom. Sliding under the covers with Martin, she tells his back, "I need a hug."

He turns and immediately wraps his arms around her. "What's wrong, sweetie?"

"Mother's driving me crazy. She's got a list a mile long for me."

"Can I help?"

Once Martin has his coffee in hand, he sits at the kitchen table with Cassie. "You'll need to stop at the drug store as well as the grocery store and the liquor store—get the keg and the ice last. See if you can recruit Gabrielle's husband Norman to help you. Take Mom's car—the keys are in it. Here, I'll draw you a map."

After finding a can of paint in the Bungalow shed, she spends the next two hours taking the wicker furniture out to the back garden and painting it there, and she grows even more irritated. She thinks of Kate and Virginia, and her blood boils in solidarity. At 11:00 a.m., Liz tells Cassie to locate a cassette recorder, so the wedding ceremony can be taped.

"Mom!" Cassie explodes. "Stop treating me like a slave!" She knows her mother is under a lot of pressure, but this is so much worse than usual. "No one's going to have a tape recorder lying around. You probably want me to come up with a slide projector too. You should have thought of that earlier."

"I don't have time for kid gloves. There's too much to do before three thirty." Liz fumbles for her cigarette pack, lights up.

Cassie replies, "You know, you could get a job where you could boss people around all day long—maybe that would make you happy."

Liz says, "I don't have time for a job. My duties as Paul's wife—"

Cassie snorts. She turns and leaves her mother standing in the back yard.

A car rolls around the wall of shrubbery and stops. Martin slides out from behind the wheel while Norman, laughing boisterously, grabs brown paper bags.

"Thanks, guys," says Cassie. "The groceries go in the Lodge, and you'll need to take the keg and the ice down to the Cottage. The folding chairs that are stacked in the living room need to go down to the Cottage too."

Martin salutes. "Yes, Mother."

"I am *not* your mother."

"Thank God," he exclaims.

"You're right. I don't want to be your mother. I don't want to be *my* mother either." Then she asks him, "Am I as bossy as Mom?" Maybe she is sometimes.

"Once in a while. I can handle it." He starts walking up to the Lodge.

Norman grabs the rest of the groceries.

She says, "I've got to check on what's happening at the Cottage."

She starts down the path. Guests are out swimming in the bay now. On her way past the Bungalow, she sees her father and Nanny on the porch. "Morning," she calls to them, waving.

"Come join us," Nanny says.

"Can't right now, Nanny. I'll stop by a little later."

"Do," Nanny insists.

Cassie finds Gabrielle in the kitchen washing dishes, her son pushing a toy truck around her feet.

"Good morning!" Gabrielle says.

"How are you today?"

"We're fine," Gabrielle replies. "Norman had a marvelous time talking with your father last night. I hope I get a chance myself today. It can be a little tough when Luke's hanging on to me." She ruffles the boy's hair, and they exchange a secret smile.

The screen door in the living room slams. A moment later Grace appears, her large straw hat weaving as she maneuvers a tray stacked with quiches onto a counter.

"Whew, it's hot!" Grace exclaims. "I hope we can get all these in the fridge." She opens the door.

"Here, let me help," says Cassie.

Taking Luke by the hand, Gabrielle backs out of the way.

After Cassie and Grace wrestle the quiches into the old Kelvinator, Grace straightens up. Smiling at Luke, she asks, "Who have we here?" When he doesn't reply, Grace looks at Gabrielle.

"This is my son Luke. I'm Gabrielle. My husband went to school with Steven."

"Ah. I'm Cassie and Penny's Aunt Grace." Then Grace addresses the little boy. "Did you get here last night?"

Luke nods.

"We came from California, so it was a long day for him," Gabrielle says.

"That *is* a long trip. Did you fly on an airplane, Luke?"

"Yes," Luke says shyly.

"Did you have a good time on the airplane?" Grace persists.

The screen door bangs again. "Hello?" Liz calls loudly.

"We're in the kitchen," Cassie replies.

Liz charges in. Very pink-cheeked, she brushes a lock of damp hair back from her forehead. "I need you at the Lodge, Cassie—we've got to set the bar up. I'll be back down in a little while, Grace, to see what I can do for you."

"No rush, Liz. We've plenty of time."

Soon Cassie is helping her mother at the front of the Lodge.

As they move the glasses and the booze, Liz remarks, "I want you to stick with the photographer. Make sure he gets shots of everyone in our family."

"That's enough!" Cassie says.

Without waiting for her mother to reply, Cassie trots down the road for thirty yards. Then she cuts in toward the water and makes her way gingerly over sharp-edged eelgrass to a solitary outcropping of granite: Pirate Rock. She finds a nook where she can't be seen. This is where, at the age of nine, she and Christopher compared garbled versions of the facts of life. When the slab of black rock under her feet begins to burn her soles, she moves down toward the cool wet sand.

The tide is going out. Walking onto the beach, Cassie is appalled to see how much garbage litters the area; bits of plastic and beer bottles are mixed in with the carcasses of small crustaceans and other detritus. The beach didn't used to be like this.

In the distance, she spots Christopher heading toward the point. She calls, "Hey, wait up, Chris!"

Christopher stops and watches her approach. "What's happening?"

"I'm on the verge of killing my mom. She's been bossing me around all morning. She gives me orders as if I'm her personal maid."

"So, what else is new? She's always been like that, hasn't she?"

Swinging her foot back, Cassie intends to boot an empty shell into the water, but she misses the periwinkle and stubs her toe against a rock instead. "Shit! Shit!" She hobbles over to a flat-topped hunk of granite at the edge of the beach. Sitting, she holds her foot in her lap. Christopher joins her there.

He says, "I remember one time when our mothers planned to take us on a picnic and your mother sent a list with you of all the things she expected my mother to bring—deviled eggs, a jug of lemonade, and so on. My mother and I just laughed. She packed potato chips and other items she knew we'd like."

"Your mother's fun. Whereas my mother treats me like shit, she really does. And she's so damned critical; whatever I do, it's never good enough. She takes me completely for granted. When my sister does a fraction of what I do for her, she gets heaped with praise, but not me, oh no, not good-old reliable Cassie."

"Liz knows she can count on you, Cassie. You're dutiful and trustworthy."

"Those qualities are boring."

"Well, I can assure you, *you're* not boring." Lightly he touches the tip of her nose with his finger.

She leans into him. "You know what I think, Chris?"

"No, CayCay, tell me what you think." He takes her hand.

He is so warm . . .

"I don't believe her life is challenging enough for her. If there isn't enough to do, she'll manufacture something. Martin doesn't agree with me on this, but he doesn't know my mom as well as you do."

Christopher says, "Moms muck along like the rest of us. Of course, they were the world to us once, when we were little."

Cassie remembers the look she saw Gabrielle and Luke exchange earlier. "Right? When you're little maybe you're in love with your mom. And hopefully she's in love with you too. But then eventually you fall out of love with each other when another child is born or whatever else occurs to separate you. Do I get so angry with her because I'm still furious at Mom for letting that happen?"

"I don't know about that," says Christopher.

"I want more time to myself so I can read Aunt Kate's diaries. She's fascinating, and I feel like I have things to learn from her. It's hard for me to focus on this wedding when I'd rather spend time with Aunt Kate."

"Tell me about her."

"Besides being a cartoonist for the suffrage movement, she was very involved in the organizing work of the Massachusetts office of the American Woman Suffrage Association. At some point she worked on birth control, but I haven't had a chance to read anything about that yet. I love learning that she was politically active. She's inspiring!"

"She sounds very modern."

"Actually, I feel like she's a friend. I think of her as Kate, not Aunt Kate, I suppose because of the intimacy I feel with her from reading her diaries."

"That's interesting."

Cassie glances at her watch. "Ugh. It's nearly noon!" She withdraws her hand from his. "I've got to get back."

In front of the Lodge she winds around groups of guests, smiling, but she doesn't stop. On the porch Martin and Steven sprawl on one of the couches with hot faces, sodden T-shirts glued to their chests. Their tennis rackets are leaning against the wall.

Steven rises. "I'd better go catch a quick shower."

Martin reports, "The keg is on ice and ready to go."

"Thank you. I'm glad you had a chance to get some tennis in," Cassie replies. She appreciates the fact that he's competitive.

"Steven and I each took a set, seven to five and six to eight, before we had to give up the court."

"So, you were evenly matched." Putting her hand on his shoulder, she says, "That must have been fun."

He nods. "It was."

She steps to the side. "Have you seen Mom?"

"Not since we got back. Maybe she's down at Nanny's."

"I should go find her."

"Sweetie, how can I help?"

"I think we're in good shape. Shower if you like."

Cassie heads down to the Cottage. The wind is teasing little whitecaps out in the bay. Gulls wheel, and she sees her father striding back and forth near the edge of the cliff, his head bent over a book. When he looks up, Cassie waves, but he doesn't respond. Then she notices his lips moving and realizes he is preparing for the wedding service. She smiles to think he feels the need to practice something he must have done a hundred times. Has he started to worry about his memory? As far as she can tell, there's nothing wrong with her father aside from his concern that his congregation might want him to retire.

As she descends the hill, Cassie spots her grandmother, reading alone on her porch. She looks good, her cheeks the same brave pink as her linen dress. "Nanny," she calls, "is Mom there?"

"She's at the Cottage with Grace."

As Cassie steps onto the Bungalow porch, Nanny puts down her *New York Times*. "Tell me what you've been up to this morning."

Cassie sits down and drags a crumpled pack of cigarettes out of her pocket. After lighting up, she says, "Well, first I hosed down the porch because it smelled terrible. Then Mom insisted that I give all the wicker chairs a fresh coat of white paint because she thought they looked grubby. I hope they dry in time. I'd hate to think our guests could stick to their chairs."

"Oh my," Nanny replies, "that would not be good."

"Meanwhile, Martin and Norman were dispatched to do the errands. Mom and I wrestled the wedding presents into the living room, and we set up the bar at the Lodge for later."

Nanny chuckles. "I feel tired just hearing about it all."

"I haven't gotten to fixing the flowers yet. They're kind of droopy."

"Would you like me to take a look at the flowers?"

"That would be great, Nanny."

Then Nanny leans back in her rocker and says, "I've been thinking about something Charlotte said the other day. She has theories about the Reed women. I don't go along with all of them . . ."

"Like what?"

"She says the women in this family are unusually strong. I'm not sure I agree. I know we live to a ripe old age. I think we're a heady bunch. I told Charlotte so."

"What do you mean by 'heady'? Do you mean we're headstrong?"

"No, I think we're driven by what we think, not by what we feel."

Cassie says, "In her diary, Aunt Kate seems to struggle with her emotions."

"How old was she when she wrote that diary?"

"Good question. I think she was pretty young during the period I've been reading about."

Nanny says, "I've always prided myself on leading with my brain, but that isn't helping me any longer. I just don't know what to do with all these feelings. I'm overwhelmed."

"Of course you are, Nanny. You're grieving."

"I don't know how to get through this."

"I bet you're doing exactly what you need to, Nanny. Crying. Talking a little."

"Well, that's enough for now. I'm sure your mother wants you down at the brunch."

Instead of hurrying down to the Cottage, though, Cassie returns to the bedroom to read just a little bit more. Nanny's not the only one feeling overwhelmed. Cassie can't face the wedding brunch quite yet.

May 23, 1915: Back in stride with Virginia again. Today I presented her with the best cartoon I have been able to draw, and she said it was stunning. Entitled "The Next Rung," the cartoon shows an ordinary barefoot woman climbing a ladder up from Ignorance and Greed to Progress. The rungs of the ladder are labeled Education, Property, Professions, Business, Votes for Women, and then at the top, True Democracy. Demons of Prejudice and Blind Injustice attempt to stop her with their spears, but they are not successful; she is reaching toward the vote.

Virginia advised me to send the cartoon to the *Woman's Journal*, for she is certain that they would publish it. She said "The Next Rung" is so good that I must create more cartoons, and the thought of trying more is most exciting. I believe that I have discovered the true outlet for expressing my convictions—at last!

<u>May 26, 1915:</u> As the sole female apprentice at Rousseau's atelier, I found out how very lonely I could be without the companionship of other women. That was a time when I desperately needed a woman friend.

Now I am discovering the inexpressible comfort women can offer to one another. While it is not always an easy matter for me to speak from my heart to anyone outside my family, whenever I do so to one of my comrades, I have found compassion and understanding; I have felt much less alone.

I am beginning to think that modesty and reticence, which I was taught to deem virtues, may not be such at all; they surely serve to keep others at arm's length. It seems that when we speak openly of our experiences, we begin to participate more in each other's lives and to be enriched as a result.

<u>June 1, 1915:</u> Last weekend I began a new regime of rising two hours earlier than usual to work on my cartoons, and I have been having a simply splendid time of it. The joy of drawing—the satisfaction of producing something really good—I had forgotten what great fun this can be. Knowing that my work serves such an important cause is a real source of satisfaction.

I started on this routine after Virginia and I spent an evening alone together while Del was entertaining a botanist from Kew Royal Gardens. Virginia and I had the most delightfully intimate conversation: I found myself confiding my childhood dreams, and I told her about studying in Paris.

Del is very impressed by my cartoons. He said he had no idea I possess this degree of artistic ability. Hesitantly, he asked if I would consider drawing for him. He is in need of an illustrator to capture scientifically accurate renderings of ferns he discovered in Costa Rica.

Down at the Cottage, Cassie squeezes through the crush of people, passing her father and Gabrielle's husband in earnest conversation again. Her father appears pale, a white bandage on his throat where he cut himself shaving, heightening the gray tinge of his neck and jowls. Cassie sees Penny gazing into Steven's face with an expression of trust and hope, but it looks like her eyes are red. Has she been crying? Over to the side, Cassie spots Christopher dispensing drinks from the keg. He looks up, and their eyes hold for a moment. Her stomach twists.

"What a great place to get married," Steven says, sweeping his gaze across the yard.

"Liz put in an order for a sunny day, and God delivered," says her father, a glass of water in his hand. "This is a big day for us all."

Steven's mother joins them. "That's right," she says. "The weather's perfect."

Cassie steps back to include Estelle.

Estelle goes on. "I just want to say what a nice family you have. I'm so impressed with your grandmother, Cassie. She's a remarkable lady."

"A real trooper," Steven agrees.

"You've welcomed us so warmly," Estelle continues. "I feel like I'm a real part of everything."

"You *are* family now," Paul asserts. "I'm just sorry my son Matt can't be here to meet you. He's off in Bulgaria working on an archaeological expedition with one of his professors."

"Is that so," Estelle says politely.

Cassie asks, "Has your other son arrived yet? Since we've never met, I won't recognize him."

"Tommy should get here anytime now. Well, I didn't mean to interrupt." She turns away.

Martin is busy talking with Norman, so after getting herself a small plate of food, Cassie looks around.

"Cassie," calls Gabrielle.

Gabrielle and Luke are sitting apart from the rest of the party, near the hammock. Cassie joins them. Gabrielle says, "This lunch is delicious." She observes the people around them.

Instinctively, Cassie feels she can trust Gabrielle. "Can you tell me something?" Cassie looks at her lap and then up into Gabrielle's face. "What do you do with feelings that you shouldn't have?"

"I guess that depends. What kind of feelings?"

"Feelings that go against your values."

"I think you listen to your feelings, but you don't always have to act on them."

"How do you know what to do when your feelings point one way and what you're supposed to do points another?"

"Follow your heart. It will always take you the right way, even if you can't see the end of the road. You can trust your heart, Cassie. Listen to your *self*."

"But sometimes my *self* wants bad things, like cigarettes and Coca-Cola."

Shaking her head, Gabrielle laughs. "Now you're talking about appetite, not soul. All I can say is, listen to what emerges from inside of you. That's the surest guide."

"Cassie!" Grace calls. "Where's your ma?" Although her words seem innocuous, Grace's tone suggests that Cassie ought to know Liz's exact whereabouts.

Annoyed, Cassie replies coolly, "I have no idea."

"I bet she's doing something we could help with," Grace remarks.

Cassie stands. "I'll go find Mom." She gets up and tosses her uneaten lunch into a trash can, then starts toward the Lodge, but as she rounds the corner of the Bungalow, she nearly collides with her mother.

"I'm coming to remind Penny and Steven that it's almost time for the rehearsal. Are they still down there? Has the best man shown up yet?"

"Not that I know of."

"Well, we'll start without Thomas if we have to."

Cassie hurries back to the Cottage, where the crowd is dispersing. She finds Penny with Estelle Rose. "Excuse me," Cassie interrupts them. "Mom says it's time for the rehearsal."

She sees that Penny is staring blankly at the paper plate in her hand. "Here, Penny, let me take that." *Do I have to do everything for you?* Fuming inside, Cassie places the silverware on a cluttered tray and tosses the trash into a garbage can nearby.

She notices Christopher picking up glasses people left on the lawn. He looks at Cassie and then down at what he is doing.

Martin calls, "What are you up to?"

"I came to get Penny for the rehearsal."

"I'll finish cleaning up here," says Martin.

"Thanks, Martin."

On the road to the Lodge, Penny exclaims to Cassie, "I can't believe it's time already." She pauses. "Actually, all of a sudden I'm terrified." Clenching her teeth, she grimaces. "Is this what they mean by *cold feet*? I didn't expect to feel this way. It's not as though I'm a blushing twenty-year-old with no conception of what she's getting into. I know what I'm doing."

Cassie doesn't say anything. She remembers her own version of cold feet. The night before she and Martin married, she had a dream about running away with Christopher.

At the Lodge, Steven grabs Penny's hand. They look comfortable together in their blue jean cutoffs and T-shirts—Penny's is covered with musical notes; Steven's is from Lake Wobegon.

"Oh good, here you are," says Liz, joining them and waving Paul over. "And here's Steven's brother. You made it just in time, Thomas."

Everyone forms a semicircle facing the ocean.

Then Paul takes charge. His voice deepens into its ministerial mode. Penny's shoulders relax. Paul directs the show, motioning with outstretched arm to the places the players should come in from and go over to as he has them walk through their parts.

Once they finish the rehearsal, Cassie heads back into the Lodge to get ready. Soon this weekend will be over with and she can get back to her own life. On the porch, she finds four musicians—colleagues of Penny's from Philadelphia. They've set up their stands, and they're tuning.

Upstairs, Cassie showers. As she dries herself, the first notes of the "Trumpet Voluntary" ring out loud and stately. Then the French horn stops, but after a brief pause, the musicians play on.

Cassie puts on the long pale pink cotton dress she bought for this occasion and then her makeup and sandals.

Penny bursts into the room. "Help me get ready, Cassie? I just have to take a quick shower first."

"Mom told me you're wearing her wedding dress, just like I did."

"Yes, but she had it shortened so it's not so fancy."

"Cool. I'll be down in a minute." Cassie puts on lipstick, blots her lips on a Kleenex, and then walks down to Penny's room.

She looks out the bedroom window as the guests begin to assemble. An old woman moves stiffly into a chair with assistance from a younger man. Cassie cranes to see. It must be Nanny's sister—Great Aunt Charlotte; the woman's face is hidden by a large hat.

While Penny dons her underwear, she says, "This is so exciting!"

Cassie is starting to feel exhilarated too. "You're getting married in just a few minutes!"

Soon she's fumbling with the tiny buttons and hooks on the back of Penny's wedding dress while her sister twists her hair into a bun.

"You're going to wear your hair up for Nanny?"

"It's better in this weather; it is so hot and sticky. Let's see how it looks with the flowers." Penny starts to jam sprigs of baby's breath into her hair.

"Here, let me."

Penny hands Cassie the flowers. While Cassie sticks baby's breath into the circumference of her bun, Penny says, "I hope Father doesn't mind doing the traditional wedding service for us. It doesn't give him much freedom, but I couldn't see having Kahlil Gibran or someone like that. No offense, Cassie. I liked your wedding, but I want something more somber. To me it feels like the old-fashioned service will provide a stronger glue for our marriage."

"It's kind of obnoxious for you to say that, Penny. Martin and I had the wedding we intended. Now you get yours."

"I said 'no offense.'"

"That doesn't erase my reaction. Never mind; this is your day. I'm sure Dad is happy to do whatever you want. Now, check out the mirror." Cassie steps back. "You look like a fairytale princess."

The baby's breath forms a light lacy crown that seems to hover above Penny's head.

"I like that effect with the flowers. Thanks, Cassie."

Feeling a rush of love for her little sister—she looks so pretty and happy—Cassie leans in to kiss her cheek.

Just then a svelte blonde looks in. Her yellow dress is so ruffled that Cassie thinks she looks like a little girl.

"Hannah!" Penny cries, rushing to hug her friend. "I can't believe you made it!"

"And not a moment too soon. Hello, Cassie." Hannah sits gingerly on the bed, looking as though she isn't sure she's welcome in the bride's bower during the time traditionally reserved for mothers and sisters and bridesmaids. Not that there are any bridesmaids.

Penny asks, "Did you just drive up from New York City this morning?"

"That's right. The traffic was horrible. There was a bad accident near Hartford, so I could only inch along for miles. Thank God I got here in time."

Penny says, "I had such a good time going to that show with you in June."

"Wasn't it great?" Hannah replies. "I've told all my friends they have to see *The Club*."

"I loved those feminists dressed in top hats, white ties, and tails. Singing naughty songs in a gentlemen's club from the turn of the century."

It occurs to Cassie that Penny probably prefers Hannah's company to her own. She turns to leave.

A trumpet sounds below.

Penny says, "This is it."

CHAPTER 7

The crowd on the front lawn begins to hush and draw together as the trumpet notes ring out. The groom and best man, dressed in navy suits and jaunty ties, stroll around the outside of the audience and join Paul, who looks wan in his white robe with gold and crimson surplice, standing with his back to the water. Paul gazes intently at Steven, then at Thomas before he moves his eyes toward the porch.

From the front rows, Liz is shooing her hands to part the people so there will be an aisle for the bride's entrance. Near Liz, Cassie sees that Nanny is sitting next to the woman with the hat. Aunt Grace and Uncle Rick take seats on Nanny's other side.

Estelle and Lester Rose stand in front of their chairs.

Cassie gives Penny one last hug.

The heat has become so heavy now that to Cassie the entire scene seems to shift into slow motion and to blur slightly. She spots the man with two cameras slung around his neck hesitating. She hurries over to him. "The bride's about to start down the aisle, so you'd better get in place near the groom."

The photographer moves to the front, and Cassie takes the seat next to Martin.

Penny's eyes are fixed on Steven the whole way down the grassy aisle as she floats through the throng. Once she reaches their father, she stops.

There is a long pause while Paul calmly surveys every face in the gathering. The photographer's shutter is clicking away.

Paul begins to speak in a quiet but penetrating tone. "Welcome, family and friends." Another long pause. Then he continues. "In the words of the poet e. e. cummings:

"love is more thicker than forget
more thinner than recall
more seldom than a wave is wet
more frequent than to fail

"it is most mad and moonly
and less it shall unbe
than all the sea which only
is deeper than the sea

"love is less always than to win
less never than alive
less bigger than the least begin
less littler than forgive

"it is most sane and sunly
and more it cannot die
than all the sky which only
is higher than the sky."

Cassie watches as Penny turns to Steven, looking worried. Cassie's glad her father is putting his own stamp on this occasion.

"In the name of the Father, and of the Son, and of the Holy Ghost. Amen. Dearly beloved, we are gathered together . . ."

While Paul intones the standard words, Cassie thinks that Penny was right to insist on a traditional ceremony. She looks out at the bay, which is so bright with ripples reflecting the pervasive sun that the wedding party dims to silhouettes. A dozen boats have moved in to watch the proceedings. Their quiet wakes set the moored sailboats rocking. Gulls circle overhead; on the rocks offshore cormorants stretch their wings out to dry.

". . . that husband and wife may give to each other companionship, help, and comfort, both in prosperity and in adversity . . ."

Sighing gustily, Nanny drops her head. Cassie watches as Charlotte gingerly places her fingers on her sister's arm and Nanny doesn't shake her off.

". . . Let us therefore invoke the blessing of God on the union now to be formed."

Martin grabs Cassie's hand and squeezes it.

"Let us pray. Almighty and most merciful Father, we your unworthy children praise you for all the bounties of your providence, and for all the gifts of your grace. We thank you especially for the institution of marriage, which you have ordained to guard, to hallow, and to perfect the gift of love . . ."

Penny wants a service that will glue her marriage together. But what glue is strong enough to ensure that a marriage will last? What happens when one partner changes but the other doesn't?

". . . and truly keep their vows; through Jesus Christ our Lord. Amen."

Raising his head, Paul gestures that Steven and Penny should step forward.

"Steven Joshua Rose, will you have this woman to be your wife, and be faithful to her alone?"

His eyes on Penny, Steven asserts heartily, "I will."

"Penelope Peters Lyman, will you have this man to be your husband, and be faithful to him alone?"

Penny whispers, "I will."

"Who gives this woman to be married to this man?"

Liz moves forward to say, "Her father and I do." Then she retreats.

"Hear the word of God in the thirteenth chapter of Paul's first letter to the Corinthians."

Cassie glances at Martin. The tennis game he played earlier has raised his color, and the jacket he chose intensifies the greenish blue of his eyes. He looks very attractive now.

"For now we see in a mirror dimly, but then face-to-face."

Christopher is standing off by himself, his nose and chin sharp against the sky. Suddenly Cassie remembers that Saturday early her sophomore year of high school, when Christopher arrived at her house unexpectedly. He'd driven his father's car down to Norwich, scooped her up, and took her out to the shore. As they walked along the sand, the sun sparkling on the water, he told her, "I know we've been friends forever, Cassie, but I think I'm falling in love with you. It's you, you're the one."

". . . but the greatest of these is love."

Then everything speeds up. Vows and rings are exchanged, several prayers are prayed, and soon it is done: Steven and Penny are husband and wife. In the exuberance of their kiss, Penny drops her bouquet. Liz steps forward to pick it up, and, winking at her daughter, she hands it back. The couple recess to the triumphant strains of Purcell's "Trumpet Tune," but before they reach the porch, the crowd dissolves into delighted cries of congratulation, and they are enveloped.

CHAPTER 8

Cassie gets a Coke at the bar and then, looking for Nanny's sister, she moves through the people onto the porch, where some of the older folks have taken the most comfortable chairs. Spotting Charlotte, she walks over.

"It's Cassie, Aunt Charlotte. I've been dying to talk with you. Nanny tells me you've been doing research on the Reed women?"

Charlotte smiles as Cassie pulls a chair around and sits. Charlotte's tanned face is deeply scored with a row of wrinkles that arc cross her forehead, and her short gray hair is curly. She seems smaller than Nanny, but maybe that's because her back is hunched. "I have. Reed women manage life by mastering the difficult, the frightening, the painful. We Reeds love to meet a challenge capably."

Charlotte is not at all what Cassie expected—she's much more direct and personal than Nanny. Charlotte's description does not seem to apply to Cassie, and maybe not to Nanny either—at least not these days. She says, "Nanny said you think Reed women are strong."

"Yes, very. And we're proud; it's difficult for us to admit that we can't do something—too proud to accept help, or even to admit need."

This resonates for Cassie. She never asks anyone for help.

"Your grandmother, when she broke her leg—it was days before she would go see a doctor and then only because her toes were turning blue."

"Ah, right," says Cassie. "I'd forgotten that."

"And your mother."

They both gaze at Liz, who is giving orders to the caterers.

Charlotte adds, "Though I can't think of any other Reed women who are religious, aside from your mother."

"I wouldn't call Mom religious. A minister's wife is expected to attend church and to be a part of the community, but if she didn't have to, I doubt she'd do any of it. I think it's hard for Mom to cram herself into the prescribed role that wives of ministers are expected to play."

Charlotte nods. "However, we are very unsure of ourselves underneath. We have a soft underbelly, for we are extremely vulnerable to our feelings, and we feel deeply. Your Aunt Grace, she's extremely bright, she graduated from Bryn Mawr magna cum laude—she could have done anything—but she never took a job. She fell in love with Rick, and that was that."

"Uncle Rick is a sexist. I'm kind of surprised Aunt Grace lets him get away with that, but maybe she doesn't want to upset the apple cart? Perhaps she muffles her talents, so she won't outshine him."

"She was very bookish as a girl." Charlotte leans forward. "I believe we're extremely passionate. We care very deeply, but we hide that. We keep all our emotions under strict control."

Cassie says, "We're passionate?"

"My daughter Harriet eloped with Ralph after knowing him one week! They went on to have six children."

Cassie pauses a moment, considering whether she herself is passionate. "Hmmm." Perhaps she is passionate. She certainly enjoyed making out. In high school she worried that maybe she was slutty because she and Christopher went a lot farther than any of her friends did. She and Chris made cautious love a few times, when many of her friends hadn't even been kissed at that point. Then she thinks about the narrowness of her parents' double bed—does that suggest *their* relationship is passionate?

"On the night of my wedding," Charlotte goes on, "Mother came to my room and shaved all the hair from my pudendum."

"What a bizarre thing to do! Like some kind of ritual an anthropologist might discover in a remote tribe somewhere."

"I figure that by making me look like a very young girl, Mother was proving that I was untouched—a virgin."

Cassie says, "I've never heard of anyone doing anything like that. Not in my women's group, not anywhere. I wonder whether this is a practice of women in other cultures?"

"Don't ever mention this to your grandmother. Mother must have done the same thing to Margaret, but we've never spoken about it. My poor husband—he must have gotten quite a shock, though he never said a word." Charlotte takes a drink from the glass in her right hand. Then she says, "Did you know I was ostracized when I started analysis?" She sounds like she's still angry.

"No."

"The family treated me as if I'd opened a can of worms. Nobody at Granite Cove would have anything to do with me. That's why we stopped coming here."

"That's terrible," says Cassie. "I never heard about that."

"Margaret still thinks I'm too psychological. Says I overanalyze everything. Well, she's just the opposite—she's afraid to look inside herself."

Charlotte seems like a kindred spirit. "What can you tell me about Kate Reed Easton?"

"Aunt Kate? She had many talents, and she was enormously competent. She could be intimidating too. She had a strict idea of everyone's place."

"Do you know what happened to her in Paris? I understand she went there to study painting, but then she gave up art and didn't paint again for years."

"Is that right? I thought she painted all her life. Painting, and working for birth control. After what she went through with that Rousseau."

"Who was Rousseau?"

"A cad. A man she studied under, in Paris. She thought he would marry her and no one would be any the wiser about her delicate condition. But she was soon disabused of that presumption."

Cassie glances around to see if anyone is listening to them. "What are you saying, exactly?"

"Aunt Kate fell pregnant. Found someone to perform an abortion. Apparently, the place was filthy, the equipment barely sanitary. She nearly died."

"How do you know so much about her, Aunt Charlotte?"

"She was a sort of mother to me. In a way, she adopted me since she didn't have children of her own."

"Why didn't Aunt Kate have children?"

"The botched abortion rendered her sterile. Aunt Kate was certainly passionate! Traveling to Paris in pursuit of a career as a professional artist and then becoming pregnant by her teacher, a Frenchman who wouldn't marry her, and then deciding to get an abortion—all while pulling the wool over the eyes of the cousin who was her supposed chaperone. Cousin Sally was mortified when she discovered Aunt Kate nearly bleeding to death in their rooms."

"Whoa." Cassie takes a deep breath. "Why haven't I met you earlier, Aunt Charlotte?"

"My husband was so furious about the family's ostracizing me that we stopped coming to Granite Cove many years ago. He refused to socialize with your grandparents. I guess your mother followed Margaret's lead—I met you at my mother's funeral in 1960, but you wouldn't remember. I was one among a blur of older folks."

"Charlotte, there you are! I've been looking all over for you." An elderly cousin in a sleeveless shift, which exposes impressive biceps, plunks down next to Aunt Charlotte.

Cassie stands. "Aunt Charlotte. May I call on you in the morning?"

Charlotte nods and then, as if she hadn't just dropped a bombshell, turns her whole attention to the newcomer.

Cassie moves toward the back garden, amazed at this extraordinary family secret. She stops to pick a little purple flower then drops it to the ground. She gazes up the hill and then down at her hands. She doesn't know what to do with herself. Maybe a drink . . .

At the bar she requests a gin and tonic, and once she has it in hand, she takes a big gulp. Then she looks for a conversation to join. She finds Nanny telling Estelle, "I might take in boarders. I like having someone to eat with. When I'm by myself, I stand in front of the refrigerator and pick at things."

The groom's mother says, "I can't imagine cooking just for myself."

Grace asks, "Do you really want to be tied down like that, Mummy? I thought you had talked about traveling?"

"Maybe it would make more sense to share the house with a friend. I don't want anyone I would have to entertain, but I'd like somebody to discuss things with over dinner."

Estelle says, "Doesn't living by yourself frighten you? When Lester's away, at night I hear noises, and I'm sure someone is breaking in."

"I never lock my doors," Nanny says. "We had a burglar once, but he was very well behaved—he took some money and went away. About twenty years later he came back, and it was the same thing all over again."

Listening to this old story, Grace and Cassie exchange a smile.

"Did he have a gun?" Estelle asks.

"Not as far as I know."

Grace and Cassie walk off together. "Mummy's amazing, isn't she?" Grace says. "I hope I'll be like her when I'm eighty. She still has great legs too." Grace points her right toe, flexing her own shapely gam.

Unfortunately, Cassie takes after her father in the legs department.

Martin joins them. "That was a nice service." He puts his arm around Cassie's waist. "Your father did a good job."

Cassie turns to face Martin. "I'm worried about him. I don't think he looks very well."

"You're imagining things, sweetie. He seems fine to me," he replies, patting her arm. Martin lurches a little. *Is he tipsy?*

Cassie steps out of Martin's unsteady embrace and reaches into her pocket for a cigarette.

Grace says, "I think I'll go load up a plate for my husband. Liz has put on a simply super spread."

As she walks away, Cassie asks Martin, "Have you had a chance to talk with Nanny's sister, Aunt Charlotte? She says Reed women are very passionate."

"Really?" He sounds skeptical.

"Her daughter eloped after knowing the guy she married for only a week—that sounds like passion to me."

"Or foolhardiness."

"They have six children."

"So?"

"And Gabrielle. Have you met her? She's Norman's wife. Gabrielle told me I don't have to live my mother's life."

"You could say that to any woman. *I* could have told you that."

"It was profound for me."

"We've had this conversation before," Martin replies.

"Yes, and I bet we'll have it again," Cassie mutters under her breath. Then aloud, she says, "I'm going to go find Helen."

Weaving through the throng, Cassie is about to squeeze by Uncle James, who's a math professor at Middlebury College, when he stops her. Nodding toward his sister, a few feet away, he says, "Liz is a marvel!"

All her mother's tension has dissolved in a glow of satisfaction as she moves around the party—her work has paid off.

"Your mother could have run Father's bank with one arm tied behind her back," Uncle James tells Cassie. "Too bad she was born a woman."

"Thank God things are different now. Today Mom could go into any career she wanted."

"As a girl, she'd be up milking the cows by six every morning, and she fixed all the machinery when it broke down. She was in charge of the operation."

Her father appears at Cassie's side. "What are you folks talking about?"

Uncle James says, "I was telling Cassie about the old days on the farm."

Paul takes a long swallow from his drink.

"Where's Aunt Barbara?" asks Cassie.

Uncle James replies, "She wanted to come, but our boys had things going on this weekend."

"How's everything with you, James?" Although Paul looks very weary, his voice is hearty.

Estelle appears at Cassie's side. "I've been wondering, how did you ever get a name like Cassie?"

"My name is really Cassandra. Dad studied Greek at Yale. He even thought about becoming a professor of Greek. That's how Penny got her name too—Penelope."

Then Cassie spots Helen talking with some older relatives. She looks hot and uncomfortable in a patterned dress that strains against her huge belly. "Excuse me," she says to Estelle, and she moves to join her cousin. "Could you use a drink, Helen? I'd be glad to get you something."

Helen says, "I'd love a tonic. Wait; I'll come with you."

As they move toward the bar, Helen says, "I can't help noticing the way you and Christopher look at each other. Whatever happened between you?"

"You don't remember? He broke up with me the summer before he went off to Berkeley. Said he thought we should be 'free to experiment,' and I was okay with that because I was worried about how much he smoked pot. I think I assumed we'd get back together."

"I thought so too."

"Things change. Life goes on."

"Cassie, I had the worst nightmare last night. Do you know if anyone in the family had a baby die or be born with something wrong?"

"Oh, Helen." Cassie takes her hand.

"I suppose lots of moms have nightmares when they're pregnant."

"If you give women an equal chance, they'll take over. They'll leave the men in the dust, and then where will you be?" Uncle Rick has materialized at her side; he shakes his finger at Cassie. "All alone, that's where."

Reluctantly, Cassie lets go of Helen's hand. Helen melts into the crowd.

"You've said as much before, Uncle Rick."

Penny's friend Hannah, standing nearby, remarks, "Some men aren't threatened by women who are their equals." Cassie smiles at her.

"My best friend's daughter is a doctor, and so is her husband," Uncle Rick says. "She works day and night while some other woman takes care of their kid. You just can't have it all."

Hannah asserts, "You're afraid we'll find out we don't need you anymore."

Uncle Rick retorts, "We do need each other. That's my point."

"Well, *I* need something to drink," says Cassie, heading back to the bar.

Hannah follows. "Men and their fragile egos. It's all because of birth control—that's the problem."

"What?" asks Cassie, after ordering a Coke.

"Birth control means men can get away with indiscriminate screwing. Now they get sex for free; we don't have any leverage for what we want. Guys will go out with you and spend the night, but they never stay for breakfast."

"Maybe you haven't met the right guy."

"I've given up. I have better things to do with my life." Casting her gaze over the assembly, Hannah says, "Besides, all the good ones are taken. Penny's lucky."

Cassie says, "They used to arrest people for passing out information about birth control."

Hannah replies, "You're kidding!"

"I'm not. I've been reading the diaries of my Aunt Kate, and she said that birth control—"

"Birth control?" Steven, who is walking past, stops to say, "Don't be talking about birth control! Having babies is the most wonderful thing in the world."

"You're not the one having them, Steven," replies Cassie. "You only help deliver them."

Hannah has started a conversation with someone Cassie doesn't know, so she exits, passing a clump of *Rosa rugosa* with wild pink flowers and reddening hips. Just beyond, she sees Nanny accosting Uncle John, who is backed up against the granite facade of the house.

"What's this I've been reading about acid rain in the White Mountains?"

"In the Hubbard Brook Valley, scientists discovered atmospheric pollution has been causing the rain to become so acidic that it is damaging trees and streams, and then people started noticing the deterioration of outdoor statues and—"

"Can't *you* do something about this? The Environmental Protection Agency is supposed to take care of things like that."

Raking his fingers through his sandy hair, Uncle John explains, "Mother, I'm doing the best I can. The EPA is only seven years old.

We're grossly understaffed and underfunded. There's only so much we *can* do. Taking on the coal-fired power industry—"

"Well, I think it's a shame." Lifting her chin, Nanny asks, "What could be more important than ensuring clean air and clean water for our great-grandchildren?"

"I couldn't agree more. We need additional resources to do the job right."

"I'll write my congressman."

"I wish you would."

Cassie moves in next to her grandmother. "Nanny," she asks, "did Aunt Kate ever paint a portrait of you?"

Uncle John looks at Cassie gratefully.

"As a matter of fact, she did. It's here in the living room."

"Really? I don't remember seeing it."

"It's not very big, but I think it's quite a good likeness."

"I'll check it out."

"Go see what you think."

The portrait, situated in a dark corner, depicts Nanny as a young woman in a deep red dress with lace at the collar and sheer sleeves. Margaret is smiling slightly, and her blue eyes are looking up, as though she's gazing at the future with confident anticipation. The details of the dress are finely wrought, but it's her grandmother's face that strikes Cassie—Kate caught Nanny's eyes and sweet expression perfectly. She's lovely, and her soft, wavy hair is brown. Cassie is touched by how hopeful Nanny appears here. She lifts the portrait off the hook to examine it more closely. It's undated but signed *KREaston*. Cassie holds the frame in both hands, thrilled that she can physically connect now with something that Kate must have spent hours creating. She savors the experience.

Then she returns the painting to its hook. How is it that she's never noticed this painting before? With all her work reading documents, has she gotten into the habit of looking down all the time? She should look up more and notice what's around her.

Stepping back, she sees that the brushwork is invisible—there's no hint of impressionism in this painting. Actually, it makes her think of the work of Robert Henri, though the background is flatter and less lively than Henri's. Did Kate ever study under Henri?

As she turns to the door, toward the laughing and conversation, she stops. She can hear Martin saying something about billable hours. The way he dismissed the very notion that she could be passionate! The air is hot, and her husband's voice only adds to her discomfort. She knows she should rejoin the party and eat a little something, but she has had enough of playing the dutiful daughter. Instead, she goes back up to her room.

CHAPTER 9

<u>August 15, 1915:</u> Back at Granite Cove for a few days, I just received a terribly discouraging letter from Del. He wrote, "I have experienced considerable surprise at your drawing of *Asplenium rutaceum*. The leaves are quite incorrect, and I am afraid the drawing must be done again. When I examined it, I considered at first the general arrangement, but now I see wherein you have made changes quite specific in character." Then he went on about the duration of the season for various plants, etc.

When will I learn to cease expending my energies in attempts to please other people?

<u>August 18, 1915:</u> The next issue of the *Woman's Journal* does not have space for a suffrage cartoon. So I called on the editor of the *Boston Transcript*, who said he would undertake to print a whole series of cartoons which will run from the first of September until the referendum November 2.

Given its large circulation, the *Boston Transcript* will be an even more effective medium than the *Woman's Journal* for educating a wide public audience about suffrage, but a whole series of cartoons will mean a great deal of work for me in the coming months. I wonder whether I have that many ideas?

First off, I want to create a cartoon that compares the equal-suffrage platform to the anti-suffrage platform. Perhaps I should try two different pedestals, instead of platforms?

Enough thinking and writing. It is time to start sketching.

<u>August 19, 1915:</u> "Two Pedestals" turned out rather well; I believe it works conceptually as well as visually. The woman standing on the anti-suffrage pedestal is attired in a fancy, fur-trimmed dress and hat, with a dog, bird, and deck of playing cards beside her. She is yawning. Her pedestal, mounted atop a curlicue labeled Ignorance, Idleness, Irresponsibility, and Inferiority, rests precariously on a small base labeled Sham Chivalry. Both the base and pedestal are beginning to crack.

To the right the equal-suffrage pedestal is a large solid block with the words Motherhood, Sisterhood, Cooperation, Service, Companionship, Love, Justice, School Vote, Red Cross, Teaching, Guardianship, Professions, and Property rising from the wide base of Education and Religion. The woman standing atop this pedestal is clothed in a plain long gown; her hands enclose her son and daughter. The contrast between the two pedestals could not be more pronounced—I trust that conveys our message!

Drawing suffrage cartoons seems to be the work that I alone can do, and it is important, useful work; it engages all of my mind and heart and spirit. Now I am thinking about a cradle—a cradle of liberty—a cradle that is big enough for both boy and girl. What would that look like?

<u>September 11, 1915:</u> President Taft responded to "Meanwhile They Drown" in today's *Saturday Evening Post*. Dear diary, listen to this! He wrote: "The implications from such a cartoon are so absurd and unjust to opponents of suffrage that they ought not to aid the cause. On the whole, it is fair to say that the immediate enfranchisement of women will increase the proportion of the hysterical element of the electorate to such a degree that it will be injurious to the public welfare."

Cassie throws down the diary; attitudes like this infuriate her. And they still exist! She can't stand being called hysterical, especially when it's unwarranted. A couple of years ago, in the seminar on the Progressive Era from 1890 to 1920, one morning before class had even started, she expressed her outrage about the fact that Aditi Sud, an assistant professor of chemistry, had been turned down for a tenure-track position despite the fact that she was recommended for the job by several university committees. Cassie wasn't yelling or crying when she stated that this was clearly a case of discrimination based on sex, but her male professor condescendingly remarked that she was behaving hysterically. She remembers looking across the table at her colleague Ann, who was clearly on her side, tears standing in her eyes. She lets the memory go, picks up the page, and continues reading Taft's comments:

"It will increase the danger of unwise millennial legislation and will promote the influence of 'organized emotion' in the conduct of our Government."

These statements are outrageous! I am tempted to answer President Taft with another cartoon: perhaps a woman suffragist on a horse that is about to bolt and an anti-suffrage female trying ineffectually to hold the straining beast back.

Outrageous is right, Kate! Cassie wonders, *Did you respond to President Taft with a cartoon of a suffragist on a horse?*

October 16, 1915: Today was a high-water mark of enthusiasm, for the suffrage parade we had organized drew hundreds of people. Even Del participated. For nearly two hours women and a few men marched up Beacon Hill, where the streets had been decorated in yellow, with flags and banners. We saw only a couple of spots of red (the anti-suffrage color) in the entire crowd. Our hard work paid off—the parade was a great success. Now we feel certain that victory is imminent.

November 3, 1915: Yesterday all our hopes were destroyed. The suffrage amendment was defeated at the polls. It was a black day in the history of the Commonwealth of Massachusetts.

Cassie looks up and says to herself, *Your disappointment must have been monumental, Kate. I can relate. Earlier this summer I went to a rally for the Equal Rights Amendment, which was first proposed in Congress by the National Women's Party more than fifty years ago. It still hasn't been ratified by enough states to become part of the Constitution.*

November 16, 1915: It appears that I had underestimated Alice. At luncheon today, she calmly informed me that she will assume the presidency of the association; the rest of the officers have consented to this plan. I felt rather wounded when I learned what had transpired without my knowledge or acquiescence.

Perhaps this is just as well—I have been so bitterly

discouraged and really seriously depleted by our defeat in
the referendum that I lack the necessary spirit to lead any
longer.

Kate, you never lacked spirit. You are the most amazing—
Cheering erupts outside. Cassie glances at the clock and is shocked
to see it's after eight. Racing downstairs, she rejoins the party just in
time to see a large group gathering around Penny and Steven, outfit-
ted now in white jeans and matching striped shirts. They hug their
parents goodbye, and people throw rice until they reach their car.
Once they're inside, Penny opens her window and blows kisses while
Steven revs the motor.

A moment later, they are gone.

As people disperse, Cassie joins her father.

He asks, "Where were you, Cassie?"

"I had to go upstairs."

"I didn't see you when they cut the cake."

"Did I miss anything else?"

Paul says, "At least Penny is taken care of now."

"Penny's very good at getting other people to take care of things
for her. Mother did all the work of this wedding, with a little help
from me."

"You know your mother likes being in charge."

"True. I'm just not sure rushing into marriage is wise. Marriage is
meant to be a lifelong commitment."

"I hope she wasn't angry about my addition to her service." Paul
glances at Cassie with bleak eyes. "Penny's still my little girl. You're
still my little girl too."

Cassie senses his sadness, but she doesn't really understand it.
She'd like to comfort him though. "You haven't lost her, Dad. She'll
be back."

Then, Martin materializes. He slides his arm around Cassie's waist. "Sweetie, let's start our own family now, too." Along with his breath, a blast of alcohol assails her.

"You know?" Cassie says.

"Your father told me." Martin puts his arms around her, and Cassie's father makes a show of leaving them alone. Martin kisses her, pushes his tongue into her mouth. "Their kid and ours can grow up together. They'd be friends."

She pulls back. "You're loaded, Martin. I'm not going to discuss getting pregnant with you while you're intoxicated. We've argued about when to have a baby for months—"

"Come on, Cassie. You aren't getting any younger."

"Stop forcing this on me, Martin."

"Forcing you! What are you talking about?" At first, he seems surprised, but then his mouth moves into a tight line. Angrily, he says, "You're just like your mother!" He releases her and walks off.

Taking deep breaths, she glances around. With all the excitement of the newlyweds departing, no one is watching her and Martin. Good. She hurries away from the others, toward the ocean. The air is thick, and it's becoming electric. Out in the bay the sailboats point at one another. The tide is near its peak.

Then she hears the tuning of acoustic guitars; she loves this part of family get-togethers. Hoping Martin will stay outside, Cassie makes her way into the living room, finds it as she hoped, crammed with cousins and guests who fill the chairs and floor. Guitar cases lean against the far wall. Uncle Rick sits ready at the piano.

Standing inside the door, her mother says, "Are we going to have music now? Hurray!"

"Have a seat, Aunt Liz."

People on the couch squeeze over to make room. Cassie tiptoes over people until she locates a space near Gabrielle. As Cassie eases herself into the corner, Gabrielle says, "Feels good to relax, doesn't it?"

"It sure does. Where's Luke?"

"In bed, sound asleep."

The music starts. Almost everyone sings along with "Here, There, and Everywhere," and a few sure voices carry the harmony. After several old Beatles tunes, one of Steven's buddies from med school calls out, "How about Aretha Franklin? Can you play 'Respect'?"

"We'll give it a try," says Ralph, a bespectacled cousin playing a Martin six-string. "What key is it in?"

"I don't know. It goes like this."

As Steven's buddy sings, Ralph starts strumming chords. When they've gone through the song once, Ralph says, "I think I've got it now. Here we go."

It's not an easy song to sing, and they've pitched it lower than Aretha's version, but he beams as he belts out the lyrics.

"Hey!" Liz shouts. "I wanna hear 'Scotch and Shoda.'"

Ralph says, "Okay, Aunt Liz."

Her mother is drunk. Cassie is in no mood to witness her behavior. She tiptoes over people again, this time heading out to the kitchen, where she lights the burner under the hot-water kettle. Suddenly ravenous, she finds some peanuts and a few pieces of cheese to eat. Once the kettle begins to scream, she takes it off the stove. When she's made her tea, she carries her mug out to the porch. On the lawn, she can see Martin and Norman. They're sitting together, facing the water. She hears Martin say, "These houses are really dilapidated compared to Nanny's place in Far Hills."

"Is that so?" Norman replies politely.

The door to the living room slams open, and Liz lurches through, her sister right behind her, saying, "Let me help you to bed." Grace puts her hand under Liz's elbow.

Liz jerks away. "Night's young. Care a myself."

Grace stays put. Liz sways as she looks around. Then she says, "Might as well. Bed." She makes her way carefully out the back.

Cassie returns to the music in the living room. After a while, she hears someone shout, "Help! We need a doctor!"

She hurries outside. People are crowding around a form lying on the grass. As Norman rushes over, he says, "Get back, everybody." After a moment, "It looks like he's had a heart attack."

Now Cassie sees that it's her father on the ground.

Norman begins to pound Paul's chest with his fist. Aghast, she is sure Norman must be breaking her father's ribs. She's terrified. Nearby, Helen says, "Uncle Paul was talking with me, and suddenly he clutched his chest and then he collapsed!"

Cassie runs to her father; Liz arrives, clutching her bathrobe. "Somebody, call an ambulance." She sounds completely sober now.

Martin appears with a large flashlight, which he trains on Paul's ashen face.

"Hang on, Paul," Liz says, gripping his hand hard.

Uncle Rick races to the phone.

All the lights in the Lodge, Bungalow, and Cottage are on now, and Nanny's silhouette is visible as she peers from her bedroom window. The throng, which keeps growing, watches helplessly. Breakers smash the rocks below.

Paul's eyes flutter open. He looks around. Squatting, Liz says, "I'm here, Paul." Wanly he smiles, his eyes holding hers like a lifeline.

Norman says, "Paul, I think you've had a heart attack. We have to get you to the hospital. You may have arrhythmia, but without a monitor we won't know for sure."

Uncle Rick returns. "I've called for an ambulance," he says.

Grabbing Cassie's hand, Martin says, "He's going to be fine, sweetie."

She reflexively snatches her hand away from him. "How do you know?" She moves closer to her father's side. She's shaking.

Finally, an ambulance pulls into the drive with flashing lights and siren. Two paramedics run over. Soon they are putting Paul into the back of the vehicle.

Liz climbs in after him, calling to Cassie, "We're going to Addison Gilbert Hospital."

"I'll be right behind you," Cassie answers.

"Bring my wallet and some clothes."

"The car keys?"

"In the ignition," says Liz.

Cassie races into the Bungalow for Liz's things. She explains to Nanny where they are going, and then she hurries into the Lodge for her glasses and contact case, which she stuffs into her purse.

CHAPTER 10

Paul is set up in the intensive care unit. Liz and Cassie wait in the vacant lounge adjacent to the ICU, whose doors caution that visiting is restricted to five minutes per hour. The lounge television blares, although no one is watching it.

When Cassie turns the TV off, Liz says, "Thank you." A smile flickers over her lips; then she returns to staring at the door.

Finally, Paul's doctor joins them. He tells Liz, "Your husband is sleeping now—we've sedated him, and we'll monitor him closely."

Cassie interrupts, "What are you giving him?"

"Morphine for pain and Xylocaine intravenously to minimize the irregularity of his heart. The next twenty-four, forty-eight hours are critical. If he gets through this period with no further incidents, he should be all right. But he's going to have to stop smoking."

"He won't like that," Liz says.

"I know," replies the doctor. "He's already informed me."

"He spoke to you?" Liz says hopefully.

"A little."

"May I see him?"

"You can look in for a minute. No visitors till morning. You folks might as well go home and get some sleep yourselves."

"I'm staying," says Liz. "I want to be here in case anything happens."

When she returns from seeing Paul, her face is gray. "He's hooked up to all these machines . . ." Dropping into a chair, she huddles in her seat.

Cassie badly wants to console her mother but senses that Liz wouldn't welcome anything that might shatter her self-control. Instead of embracing her, she stays on the couch. "Mom, he'll be all right. I know he will. We're lucky. Norman was right there, and Dad revived quickly and now they're watching him."

Liz closes her eyes.

Sudden fear for Liz and then herself grips Cassie. "Mom, can I give you a hug?"

Opening her eyes, Liz says, "All right." She doesn't move, though.

Cassie puts her arms around her mother's rigid back. "Should we call Penny?"

"On her wedding night?" Liz replies angrily. "Of course not. I'll call her in the morning."

Cassie is in the midst of a marvelous dream about Christopher when she wakes with a start. She sees her mother slumped on a couch in the ICU lounge, and then she feels sick. Really sick. Throwing up sick. She jumps to her feet and urgently searches for a toilet. Rushing into a stall, she sways over the bowl, but the nausea passes. She returns to the lounge. Quietly she removes the calendar from her purse and checks the date when her last period started. Then she feels even worse. But it's impossible. She's wearing an IUD!

Liz asks, "What time is it?"

Cassie glances at her watch. "It's 6:00 a.m., Mom. I'll go see what I can find out."

At the nursing station in the center of the ICU, a woman is writing on a chart. Ten screens mounted on the wall behind her show recumbent patients. Monitors blip.

"How's my father, Paul Lyman?"

"He had a quiet night. The doctor will come talk to you after he's taken a look at him. Dr. Barnes should be here by 7."

At 8:00 a.m., Dr. Barnes reports that Paul is stable, and his cardiac enzymes are looking better. Liz picks up the phone to call Nanny and Penny. Then Liz and Cassie go into Paul's room.

"I feel better than I have in months." Despite his pallor, Paul seems positively ebullient. "Each day of my life from this time forward will be a gift from God."

"I'm so happy, sweetheart," Liz says, kissing his hand.

"I'll be fine," Paul says. He smiles beatifically. "Why don't you all go back and speed the parting guests?"

"Are you sure?" Liz asks.

"Absolutely. They've got me so doped up I'll sleep most of the day anyway."

"All right," Liz agrees, reenergized. "I'll come back this afternoon. Let's go, Cassie."

Cassie would like to stay here at the hospital with her father, but it's such a relief to see him feeling so much better now that she starts thinking ahead. She and Martin are supposed to fly back to Minneapolis this afternoon.

Liz asks Paul's nurse to call if there's any change, and then she and Cassie leave. Liz drives briskly through the cold fog and thinks aloud about staying on at Granite Cove longer. Rain drizzles from the gray sky. Cassie doesn't know what she will do if she is pregnant—the possibility terrifies her. She says, "I'll change my plane reservation, so I can stick around until we know more."

"*Could* you? That would be great, Cassie. I'd appreciate the company."

"I'll call Northwest." Cassie wants to be helpful, and while she's touched by her mother expressing any vulnerability, she feels slightly ashamed that one of her reasons for staying is to get a pregnancy test without Martin's being aware of what she's doing.

Back at the Lodge, the porch is crowded. Leaping to his feet, Martin asks, "How is he?"

Nanny's eyes fasten on Liz as Norman asks, "What do the docs say?"

Liz replies, "He's *much* better. Paul had a quiet night, and his spirits are great. The doctor seems cautiously optimistic. The electrocardiogram shows that Paul's heart sustained some damage, but the doctor says he is stabilizing."

"That is good news," Martin replies, moving next to Cassie. She doesn't meet his gaze.

Turning to Norman, Liz says, "I want to thank you for everything you did last night." Grabbing Paul's madras jacket from the chair where he left it, she clutches the garment to her chest. "You saved Paul's life."

"I'm glad I was there. He's a good man."

"As are you," replies Liz. "Thank you." She looks at Cassie. "This place is a mess."

Cassie picks up a load of dirty glasses and mugs and carries them to the kitchen. Then she gets on the telephone.

"Hello, Aunt Charlotte?"

"Yes, dearie."

"I can't come visit you today. My father's in the hospital—he had a heart attack last night."

"No! How is he now?"

"The doctor seems pretty optimistic. But the house is still full of people from the wedding. I've got to help say goodbye to our guests, change my plane reservation—"

"Just give me a call when you know more."

"Will do. I'd like to see you again."

Then she dashes upstairs to the bathroom in their room to check her underpants. Still no blood. Her stomach tightens. *I cannot be pregnant.* After closing the door to her bedroom, she grabs the pages of Kate's diaries to calm down and focus on something that's safely in the past.

January 5, 1916: Now that I have recovered my energies, I understand that it will be an even slower, more laborious process to win the vote than I had ever anticipated, and I simply do not have the heart for it. My sense of bitter disillusionment over our defeat has passed; what lingers is a renewal of the old belief in myself as an artist.

Over the past weeks and months, the conviction has been growing upon me that I must develop my artistic power, for that is the greatest talent I possess.

This morning I plan to look in at the Boston Museum School and inquire about enrolling in a life drawing course. I feel rather giddy at the prospect of embarking upon my real work again.

June 2, 1916: I am undone. Today I saw Dr. Standish, a specialist whom Mother recommended, because I could not understand why, after three years of marriage, I have failed to conceive. Dr. Standish examined me thoroughly and he could find no physical defect. After he pressed me for all the details of my private history, he pronounced that in all likelihood my ordeal in Paris has rendered me barren. Despite the fact that he is the least sympathetic physician I have ever encountered, I burst into tears there in his office, and I am still desperate with unhappiness.

Forever childless! I can scarcely imagine. If I cannot love and nurture my own children, whatever shall I do with all the longing that fills me? I am barren—such a sad word—such emptiness. My grief is nearly insupportable.

Cassie glances up, catches her reflection in the mirror. Now Kate's diary is hiking her anxiety. There's a knock, and then Penny opens the door.

"I can't believe it. Is he really okay now?" Penny's face distorts as she bursts into tears.

Cassie rises to embrace her sister.

"How could this happen on the day of my wedding?"

Dropping her arms, Cassie replies coldly, "Dad's cardiac arrest has nothing to do with you."

"I'll never be able to look back on our wedding with pleasure." Penny sobs.

Touched then by her sister's grief, Cassie says, "I know, Penny. This is terrible." She pats the bed, inviting her sister to sit down with her.

Wiping her hand over her cheeks, Penny asks, "How's Mom doing? She was pretty curt on the phone."

"She's acting like everything's going to be fine. And it will be!"

"We're supposed to stay at a B and B near Portland. I'm going to cancel—"

"Why not visit Dad and then take your honeymoon? He's feeling fine now."

Penny shakes her head. "I don't know."

"Dad spilled the beans to Martin. About your pregnancy."

"That doesn't matter anymore."

"The thing is . . . I'm afraid I might be pregnant now. Martin doesn't know."

"You too?" Penny bounces to her feet. "That's exciting!"

"No, it isn't. I need to finish my PhD. I want to make my mark. I . . ."

Penny strokes her belly, which looks only slightly rounder than usual. "I'm enjoying pregnancy. Getting to know the little person inside me."

For Cassie, an embryo is not a baby. Life doesn't actually start until birth. "If I'm pregnant, I don't know what I would do, Penny."

Cassie discovers her mother alone in the pantry, making herself a drink.

"The sun's not over the yardarm, but I can't wait," Liz says. Suddenly she covers her face. "What if he dies?" she whispers. "I couldn't bear it!"

Cassie hugs her fiercely.

Her mother leans into Cassie for a few moments before she pulls back. "He won't die."

"Of course not, Mom. We need him to live."

"I'm not sure how much he feels needed." She shakes her head. "I'm going back to the hospital as soon as we clear the decks here."

Then Cassie finds Martin in the bedroom packing. He glances at her. "You'd better get moving. We need to leave for the airport in a few minutes."

"I'm not going now," Cassie says.

"What?"

"I can't leave while Dad's in the hospital. I've asked Aunt Grace if she can take you to the airport. I don't know how long I'll need to stay here."

He removes a white shirt from a hanger, folds it, and places it in his open suitcase on the bed. He doesn't say anything. Then, "I want you home as soon as possible."

"You can get along without me for a few days. I need to be here for my parents."

"Nanny's here."

"I'm their *daughter!*"

"I know that."

"While I'm out here, I might go back to Smith. I only scratched the surface of the stuff they have there."

"You're talking about being away for weeks!" He snaps his suitcase shut. "Do what you want, Cassie. You always do anyway."

"That's not true! I do what you want a *lot* of the time."

"I've got to go."

He slams the door on his way out. She takes some deep breaths before she moves over to the bed.

August 12, 1916: Even though a good number of us rose to his defense, Van Kleek Allison was indicted today after having been arrested for distributing obscene literature. Naturally, he will appeal.

What happened was that one evening earlier this summer when the whistle blew for closing time at the North End Candy Factory, Mr. Allison stationed himself by the exit and handed out pamphlets to the young women leaving for home. He was promptly arrested for distributing "obscene" literature, although the documents were simply entitled "Don't Have Undesired Children" and "Why and How the Poor Should Not Have Many Children."

Obscene indeed! Although condoms have been employed for many years to prevent contagious diseases, our legislators do not tolerate contraceptives for women. The obscenity statutes, following the so-called Comstock law of 1873, which forbade use of the mail for obscene, lewd, and lascivious literature, apparently pertain to contraceptive information and devices. In other words, by law, birth control is deemed obscene, lewd, and lascivious.

These laws must be changed. Married women and

prospective mothers *need* to know how to control conception. I am appalled that this information can be denied to
the women who need it most.

It's as though Kate is speaking directly to her.

October 27, 1916: Over the last two months we have become
targets of considerable abuse and notoriety. The newspapers
have printed pictures of the members of Allison's defense committee and columns of print giving details of his trial and the
offensive attacks by District Attorney Joseph C. Pelletier, who
called us "Women of the idle rich who prefer poodles to babies."

He said, "What are we to think of women who would
idolize a man pleading to such a charge, wasting hours of
their time in order to hear publicly a story unfit for any
woman's ears."

As if birth control weren't a concern for women!
According to Pelletier, birth control is onanism, which
means masturbation or incompleted coition. He implies
that the only true intercourse results in conception. That
is patently unfair! I cannot comprehend men like Pelletier,
who would make of all women brood mares. . . or slaves.

Meanwhile, along with reiterations in the press of
Pelletier's offensive remarks, we are being attacked from the
pulpit, where clergymen use their sermons to denounce our
members as a menace to society.

I do not know how to reply effectively to the extreme
emotionalism and hyperbole that the topic of birth control
seems to excite in our state. No doubt the powerful influence
which the Roman Catholic Church exerts upon the majority
of citizens in Massachusetts accounts for a great deal of this;
reason certainly cannot.

Will the obscenity statutes be used to prevent physicians and other qualified persons from applying scientific knowledge to an important human interest? Not if I have anything to say about it!

November 18, 1916: Last evening we saw the splendid play *Suppressed Desires* with our friends Peter and Crystal, whom we are visiting for the first time since they moved to New York City. Although they had not seen the play themselves, they thought it would be a good introduction to Greenwich Village for us, and so it was.

Suppressed Desires (written by George Cram Cook and Susan Glaspell, who are husband and wife) makes fun of the psychoanalytical craze that has been in vogue recently. During the course of the play, the wife is a real devotee of psychoanalysis until her doctor tells her husband that his suppressed desire is to separate from her. I relished her line about how scandalous our unconscious selves are—they do not seem at all like *us*.

I think that went right to the point: desires are one thing over which we have no control. It may be well to take notice of them, but this does not mean that we must act upon them; we are creatures of conscience after all. I dislike the manner in which the subconscious mind would seem to rob one of pride. Pride has its uses.

Cassie puts the page down. This mention of psychoanalysis makes her think about Aunt Charlotte. As soon as her father gets out of the hospital, she will make a point of visiting with her.

But if she's pregnant? What will she do? Start a family with Martin? Is this something she could discuss with Aunt Charlotte? She appears to be unshockable. On the other hand, how does Aunt

Charlotte feel about conception? She didn't seem to hold it against Kate. *I cannot be pregnant; that's all there is to it.*

<u>November 24, 1916:</u> I fear that Del has gone off the whole idea of "the new woman" because of Crystal, although I, at any rate, thoroughly enjoyed our visit to Greenwich Village. I was delighted to become acquainted with the women and men there who are attempting to remake the fabric of American society by creating in their own lives a revision of all the attitudes and customs concerning the sexes. If they have their way, a revolution of the entire social contract will result. I wish them every success.

Their ideologies of free love and socialistic redistribution of wealth are too extreme, but I suppose that they must take a dramatic position if they are to be noticed. And the proposal for community apartments, where trained professional workers would provide the services of housekeeping, cooking, and caring for the children, goes to the very heart of the matter, for then women will be freed to pursue their own particular work instead of having to become homemakers if their talents do not lie in that direction. Wealthy women have always had the advantage of such services; why not make them affordable for women in less favorable economic circumstances as well? I think it's a marvelous idea. Of course, information about ways to limit family size, which the well-to-do possess, would also be readily available to anyone who wants it.

Crystal asked why fidelity is expected only of women, not of men—it is hardly fair. She said women cannot become whole, fulfilled human beings until they break loose from society's sexual and social restraints. She claimed that Freud has amply demonstrated the need for sexual fulfillment, but until women heed their own sexual desires, they will not truly become the equals of men.

These words, written more than sixty years ago, remind Cassie of Erica Jong's rowdy novel again, which was remarkably uninhibited in its depiction of Isadora Wing's sexual adventures. Will the current sexual revolution finally achieve true equality for women?

At that juncture, I reminded Crystal that without birth control, women cannot afford to heed their sexual desires. She waved my objection away, intimating that birth control was a petty detail in the face of her grand philosophy, so I informed her that for the women of Massachusetts, access to contraceptive information is anything but assured.

During our train ride home, Del and I argued about free love. I contend that the new feminists are wise to incorporate men and love into their program because the suffragists neglect to include men; as a result, society views suffragists as bluestockings who have no use for the male of the species—a misapprehension that puts off many who might otherwise have been converted.

November 27, 1916: Today the Birth Control League of Massachusetts, which grew out of the committee for Van Kleek Allison's defense, formally adopted its first constitution, elected officers, and invited twenty well-known people to comprise an advisory board. I shall serve as president; Doctor Mabel Austin Southard, a lecturer on birth control, and Mr. Prescott F. Hall, an attorney, were elected vice presidents; and Mr. Stuart Chase will be treasurer. Legislative change is our first order of business.

<u>January 11, 1917:</u> Yesterday the suffragists began to silently picket the White House because their delegations to the president and lobbying congressmen had not produced any results. This is the first time in history that the White House has seen pickets at its gates. The "Silent Sentinels" held banners proclaiming "Democracy Should Begin at Home," "Mr. President, What Will You Do for Woman Suffrage," and "How Long Must Women Wait for Liberty?" How long indeed!

<u>January 15, 1917:</u> All twenty-five legislators whom we approached as possible sponsors of our bill have refused. The more conservative members of the Birth Control League believe now that we should engage in active educational work through meetings, individual conferences, and circular letters before we try the legislative route again. I objected on the grounds that education proceeds too slowly—I believe we should find some means of dramatizing the problems that birth control can alleviate—but I was overridden. We shall launch an educational campaign instead.

What about some cartoons about birth control to dramatize the problems, or have you had enough of drawing cartoons on behalf of your cause, Kate?

<u>January 30, 1917:</u> Yesterday, decision was reserved on Margaret Sanger's trial for operating the first birth control clinic in America, which opened three months ago at 46 Amboy Street in Brooklyn, New York. Last night a meeting was held at Carnegie Hall, and according to today's *New York Times*, "Three thousand persons in mass meeting last night started a concerted movement for the repeal of the law

forbidding the dissemination of birth control knowledge . . . Mrs. Margaret Sanger made a speech in which she threw all caution aside and removed all doubt as to her purpose when she declared that she had devoted her life to the cause of voluntary motherhood, and would continue to fight for birth control, courts or no courts, workhouse or no workhouse." Apparently, the crowd answered with wild cheers. This is the sort of dramatic publicity that our league must attract.

I like Margaret Sanger's term "voluntary motherhood"— its meaning is clear and more positive in tone than "birth *control*," which has connotations of restraint that some might find distasteful. I shall try to persuade Mrs. Sanger to come speak to our organization.

Voluntary motherhood. Every woman should be able to choose whether she wants to become a mother and when. *If* she is pregnant, Cassie will have to stay with Martin. It would be the end of working on her dissertation, at least for a while. Even if she leaves Martin, a child would tie her to him forever. As a strong sense of revulsion rises in Cassie, her stomach tightens into a hard knot, and then she gags. Now she understands all she needs to know about her marriage.

CHAPTER 11

By Monday morning, life seems to have settled down. Paul is recovering at the hospital. Penny calls to report that she had a good visit with him before she and Steven left for their honeymoon. Liz departs to see Paul and get an update from his doctor. By 9:30 a.m., Cassie is free to go visit Charlotte, who gives her directions over the phone. She heads out to the road that runs along the perimeter of Cape Ann and continues for five minutes until she comes to the driveway marked 140. As she walks up to the front of the house, she sees a sign over the door that reads *The Studio.*

"Hello! Aunt Charlotte?"

A moment later Charlotte peers through the screen door. "Come in, come in!"

Cassie steps inside.

Charlotte is wearing a wrinkled cotton shirt and purple pedal pushers—an outfit Nanny would never be seen in. The room has windows on two sides and a large skylight to the north.

"I can see why this is called the Studio."

Charlotte motions Cassie toward one of two wicker chairs that face each other. "It's off the beaten path," she comments. "Aunt Kate valued her privacy when she came here."

Taking a seat, Cassie replies, "This was Aunt Kate's place?"

"I bought it from her before she died. I love all the light. It cheers me right up." She eases into the other chair.

"It almost seems like I can smell oil paint."

"I know; it must be embedded into the floor and walls." Charlotte leans forward. "Now tell me all about your father."

"Late Saturday night, after Penny and Steven left for their honeymoon, Dad suddenly collapsed while he was talking with Helen. Fortunately, one of Steven's physician friends was nearby, and he provided emergency treatment for what turned out to be a heart attack. We called an ambulance, and Dad was taken to Addison Gilbert. He's still there. Mother just left to be with him. The doctor told us the first forty-eight hours are critical."

"I hope he recovers quickly."

"Me too."

"Now tell me about you, Cassie."

"I'm a graduate student in history at the University of Minnesota, specializing in women's history. I got my master's degree, and I've started looking for a topic about which to write my dissertation."

"Good for you! Are there other women in your graduate program?"

"Most of the graduate students in history are men. One woman who started with me let it be known that she hoped to write historical children's books. She was gone after the first semester. I guess our professors didn't think she was serious enough."

"What attracts you to Aunt Kate?"

"I find her very inspiring. I love that she was involved in founding the Birth Control League of Massachusetts—she certainly was passionate about that. I'm thinking I might be able to frame my dissertation around her work on behalf of birth control."

Charlotte says, "Apparently during a demonstration on Newbury Street in Boston around 1913, she went around handing out condoms. Her nephew told me that."

"I wish I'd known her!"

"She was a character. When I was struggling with my marriage and went into analysis, most of the family shunned me, but Aunt Kate suggested I study psychology. I ended up working as a psychiatric social worker for three decades."

"Wow! That must have been interesting."

"It was—very."

"Now I understand why Nanny isn't all that comfortable with you."

"We play out the usual older-sister-younger-sister dynamic."

"You're younger than Nanny?"

"Two years younger. Our brothers came after us." She shifts in her seat. "Once you have your degree, do you plan to teach?"

"Yes. Fortunately, there are quite a few colleges in the Twin Cities area. I hope one of them will hire me."

"I bet they will."

"Unfortunately, I'm afraid I might be pregnant."

"You'll want to find out for sure right away. A few weeks ago, I read in The New York Times that some pharmaceutical company has just released a pregnancy test that can be self-administered at home. You should ask at the pharmacy in Gloucester."

"I didn't know that—thank you for telling me, Aunt Charlotte. I'll check it out." All of a sudden, Cassie gets a scared feeling about her father. "I should go, Aunt Charlotte."

She hurries back to the Granite Lodge. Her mother hasn't returned from the hospital, so she goes over to Nanny's and looks for the keys to her father's car.

At the hospital a nurse tells her that her mother just left. Cassie goes into her father's room. He's asleep. She pulls a chair up next to his bed, so she can gently take his hand and hold it. When she squeezes it, he squeezes back, and even though he doesn't open his eyes, she feels comforted by his response. After sitting quietly with him for some time, she gets up.

As she drives into Gloucester past the Friendly's ice cream shop on the rotary, the street seems even more crowded than she remembers. Cars and delivery trucks are parked on both sides, so there's barely enough room for two vehicles to pass each other going in opposite directions. Many of the narrow houses are white-painted clapboard with steep roofs, granite blocks defining small gardens in front. There are cafés, a fish shop, and some bars along the street. Eventually the road winds around Our Lady of Good Voyage Church (a Mission Revival structure with two towers topped with one cross each) and then down to the harbor.

Cassie parks along Main Street and walks up one block to the Cape Ann Pharmacy. When she opens the door, a bell tinkles. Entering, she's surprised by how medicinal the place smells—is that odor isopropyl alcohol? She walks past a small display of gum and candy cigarettes, then along an aisle filled with Band-Aids, hydrogen peroxide, and other first aid items, then aspirin, Bufferin, Tums, and Coricidin. When she sees that there's a customer at the counter in back, she wanders along the aisle, pretending to examine the various hair dyes and rinses on the shelves. She's embarrassed, doesn't want anyone to overhear her request. When the customer turns to leave, she approaches the pharmacist.

He's an elderly gentleman in a white coat with gold wire-rimmed glasses and a sharp nose.

"Yes, miss, how can I help you?"

She notices a selection of Trojan condoms right behind him.

Taking a deep breath, she says, "I understand there's a new product—a pregnancy test that can be administered at home. Would you have one of those?"

"The sales rep brought in something a few weeks ago—it's called a Predictor. Is that what you want?"

"May I take a look?" She reaches out with her left hand so he'll spot her wedding ring.

Turning his back, he leans down to a lower shelf. When he offers her the clear plastic box labeled Predictor, she takes it. Inside she can see an eyedropper with a blue rubber top, a test tube with a blue stopper, and a small mirror. She figures the test tube must have some chemicals inside.

He says, "I don't know how reliable this is."

"I'll buy it." She gives him a twenty-dollar bill, again using her left hand.

He returns three quarters to her and slides the box into a plain white bag, which he places on top of the counter.

"Thank you." She can't wait to get out of there. She hurries down the store's other aisle, with its displays of nail polish in shades of red and pink, mascara and eye shadow by Maybelline and Almay, eye drops and saline solutions.

As she drives along winding Route 127 back to the Lodge, Cassie hardly notices the cawing of gulls or the saltwater scent of the air. She parks behind the Lodge so Nanny and her mother won't know she's back. Since it's early afternoon, they're probably in bed taking their naps anyway.

Up in the bathroom, she opens the clear plastic box. A small piece of paper slips out, instructing her to squeeze a few drops of urine into the test tube. First, she has to find something to collect her urine in, so she returns to the kitchen for a small bowl, which she holds under her bottom while she pees.

Once a little urine is in the test tube, the instructions tell her to peer through the transparent wall of the box at the mirror just below the tube. In its reflection she can watch the bottom of the test tube, where a compound will react with the drops. If in two hours a red circle appears, she is pregnant.

Cassie puts the plastic box on her bedside table and lies back against a pillow to wait. She picks up some pages from Kate's diaries.

March 6, 1918: I could have wept with longing when I held baby Lucia in my arms this afternoon—her sturdy little body was so soft and warm as she snuggled against my breast. The poor girl had fallen and hit her head on the floor, and then after several awful moments of silence, she started to cry so hard that I flew to her and picked her up before my sister could put down her knitting. Once Lucia had had quite enough of comforting, she squirmed to get down. I could hardly bear to let her go, but I released her, feeling as though my heart were being torn from my chest.

I realize that I have not yet reconciled myself to childlessness, and I must confess that I have been avoiding Evelyn's children, probably out of some mistaken notion of self-protection, but that is foolhardy—I do not need to deprive myself of the company of children simply because I can have none of my own. Indeed, I would dearly love to play a more active role in the lives of my nieces and nephews.

So, I shall. My efforts on behalf of the Birth Control League of Massachusetts have not borne much fruit yet, and they do not absorb all of my time. Neither does painting—my recent work of copying old masters is merely an exercise, after all.

Cassie closes her eyes. When she opens them, she sees the red circle in the test tube. She starts to shake. She doesn't long for a baby she can hold against her chest, the way Kate does. Maybe she will someday, but not yet.

She has to figure out what to do. Soon. She has—what? Maybe two or three weeks to get a legal abortion? If that's the route she's going to choose. If she can trust this test; if she truly is pregnant.

A wave of nausea hits her. Cassie moves cautiously down to the kitchen, where she finds some saltine crackers. Chewing them as she stands at the sink, she recalls that Coca-Cola is supposed to calm an upset stomach. She opens the refrigerator door and pulls out a glass bottle of Coke. She takes a swig, and then she decides she really needs to know for sure whether she's pregnant or not.

Going back outside, she climbs into her father's car and drives to the hospital. At the front desk when she asks for the lab, she's directed to a room in the basement. She talks the young technician into testing a sample of her urine, and while she waits for the official results, she thinks about her father. She'd like to go up and see him again, but she knows he'd be able to tell right away that something is wrong. She doesn't want to upset him. She picks up a copy of *The Boston Globe* from a nearby table and reads that Elvis Presley was found dead in the bathroom at Graceland at age forty-two. That's awfully young to die.

When the tech confirms that she is indeed pregnant, Cassie hangs on until she reaches the sanctuary of the car, but then she bursts into hoarse, choking sobs. Once she's able to catch her breath, she returns to Granite Cove. It's almost time for the cocktail hour, so she goes up to her room to change into a skirt and a comfortable oversized collared shirt she likes. Will her mother and Nanny notice that her eyes are red and swollen? *What am I going to do?*

On her way down to the Bungalow, she grabs another bottle of Coke, which she nurses while Nanny and her mother drink their whiskey on ice. Nanny reports on the tent guys, who came and removed their equipment, and on someone from the catering company, who took the last of their gear.

Liz says, "How are we going to transport all those wedding gifts?"

Cassie stares out at the ocean. Maybe she should give her baby to Penny, who could raise her own child along with Cassie's—pass them off as twins. Could she do that?

"I'm sorry, Nanny, Mother, will you excuse me? I'm not feeling well."

"Don't you want something to eat?" Liz asks.

"No. Thank you. I'm going to bed."

"Let me know if you need anything, dearie."

"I will."

At 5:00 a.m., Cassie hears the telephone ring next door. She jerks awake, and with a fearful sense of foreboding, she hurries down to the Bungalow. Her mother stands inside the door, holding the receiver. Her lips are white. "It's the hospital. Your father has died. He had another heart attack." Her voice starts to wobble when she says, "They tried to revive him but . . ."

"Oh, Mummy." Cassie hugs her mother hard.

CHAPTER 12

Cassie feels as if she's in a dream while she returns to the Lodge and numbly pulls on some jeans and a shirt. Then she drops into a chair, stunned. Her father *can't* be gone. He was all alone. Did he die in his sleep, or was he aware of being alone? Why wasn't she there with him? He loves her unconditionally. *Loved* her. Will she ever experience love like that again?

A few minutes later, she and Liz take off for the hospital.

While Liz speaks with the staff in the ICU, Cassie goes to sit with her father. Paul is laid out on the bed with a sheet covering him up to his shoulders. He looks like an extremely accurate wax version of himself. All the monitoring equipment has been removed from the room, so it's quiet. Cassie takes her father's hand—it is heavy and cold. "I'm sorry, Dad; I'm so sorry I wasn't here with you." Tears stream down her cheeks. "I hope you weren't scared." She leans over and rests her head on his chest. "Daddy. What am I going to do without you?"

It's after 8:00 a.m. when her mother begins driving them back to Granite Cove. Cassie should call Martin—tonight. She'll tell him about her father but nothing else.

Sitting very tall, Liz's body is stiff, her jaw tight. Cassie thinks that if she touches her mother right now, she might shatter.

"First thing when we get back to Granite Cove," Liz says, "I've got to get on the horn to Harry Bradshaw to have him send a hearse for Paul's body. Then the church. We'll hold the memorial service on Saturday—that way Penny and Steven won't have to cut their honeymoon short. Will you call Penny, Cassie? And see if you can send a telegram to Matt."

"What are you thinking, Mom? Once she hears about Dad, will Penny want to continue her honeymoon?"

"I don't know." Liz blinks rapidly.

Has her mother cried yet? "What's going to happen with Dad's body?"

"Cremation, of course. We discussed that ages ago."

As soon as they get out of the car, Cassie goes up to her room in the Rock Lodge and crawls under the covers. She feels gutted. She cries for so long her eyes are nearly swollen shut.

Eventually Cassie overhears her mother downstairs. "Harry? It's Liz Lyman. I'm calling from Massachusetts. I need you to send a hearse up here right away to collect my husband's body."

Cassie flinches at her mother's tough way of talking about her father.

"Yes, Paul Lyman. He died early this morning." There's a pause. Then Liz replies, "Wednesday, then. He's in the morgue at Addison Gilbert in Gloucester."

The morgue. She gets a chill thinking of her father there.

A few moments later, Liz says, "I need to speak with Jeremy Fisher." Another pause. Then, "Jeremy, Paul has died. We'll want a memorial service this weekend. What about Saturday? You have a wedding in the sanctuary that morning? I think we'll need the sanctuary. Saturday afternoon, then? Two o'clock?"

Cassie wanders downstairs. Her mother is sitting at a table with the telephone in the Lodge's dining room, the cord stretched to its full length.

"Why are you making all these calls from here instead of the Bungalow, Mom?"

"I don't want to upset Nanny any more than necessary."

What about me?

"So, the memorial service will be on Saturday?" Cassie asks.

"Yes."

Next Liz calls directory assistance to get the number for the Norwich Garden Florists. "I'd like to order flowers . . ."

Cassie recalls the bouquet Penny carried just three days ago. This is too much. Running upstairs to the bathroom, she retches into the toilet. It feels as though her body is trying to expel the fetus that has started to grow inside her.

Once her body settles down, Cassie tries to reach Penny at the B and B where she and Steven are staying. The woman answering the phone there takes a message. Next she calls the archaeology department at Cornell University, where her brother Matt is an undergraduate. The departmental secretary provides her with an address in Bulgaria she can use to cable her brother. Then she telephones Northwest Orient Airlines and books her return flight back to Minneapolis on Sunday. She telephones her Planned Parenthood office to make an appointment for Monday. She calls Ann, whom she met in the first women's history course she took at the U on women in the Revolutionary Era. The title of the course tickled her: "But What Have I to Do with Politicks?" She and Ann have been fast friends ever since.

"Ann, will you be around next week? I might need your help."

"I'll be here. What's going on, Cassie?"

"I just found out that I'm pregnant."

"Whoa!"

"I'm not sure I want to go through with this pregnancy, but Martin will hit the roof if I don't. Could I come stay with you for a few days if I need to?"

"Of course. Where are you?"

"I'm still out east. My father died."

"Oh, no!"

"I know. I can't believe it."

"I'm so sorry, Cassie. Call me whenever, day or night."

"Thank you, Ann."

Exhausted, Cassie gets into bed and sleeps for hours.

When Cassie joins Nanny and Liz for supper, she sees that her mother's eyelids are pink. Silently, they eat the poached eggs on corned beef hash that Nanny prepared.

Finally, Liz asks, "Did you reach Penny?"

"Not yet. I left a message for her to call."

"Your father was looking forward to grandchildren so much. He was delighted by Penny's news." Then, as if speaking to herself, Liz says, "Actually, I have mixed feelings. Getting pregnant derailed my life. It was never my plan to marry."

"What?" Cassie is stunned. "You didn't want me?"

"You needn't go into all that, Liz," Nanny says. "It was a long time ago."

"I wanted to run the bank my great-grandfather founded," Liz says, sounding defensive.

"That's not something to tell the daughter who changed your life," Nanny insists.

"I embraced motherhood eventually."

"You were pregnant before you and Dad married?" Cassie asks.

"That's right."

"But how . . ."

"How do you think, Cassie? I'm not the Virgin Mary. Paul and I got carried away."

"But—"

"Enough about this. Did you send Matt a cable?"

"I called his archaeology department and got an address, but I haven't sent the cable yet. It's not as though he'd be able to get home in time for the service."

Liz looks like she's about to fall apart; she pulls out a cigarette and lights it with a trembling hand. Then she rises. "I need to get to bed." She starts for the stairs. Without glancing back, she adds, "You write the obituary, Cassie. I'm no good at that sort of thing."

Cassie stares after her mother, speechless. She looks at Nanny. "I had no idea . . . I'm in shock," she manages, before she drops her head and tears splatter her cheeks.

"We all are," Nanny replies. "Death is so damned final."

In her room, Cassie pulls out a large notepad and pen from her L.L.Bean bag and starts to write: *Reverend Paul Norwood Lyman, age fifty-five, died suddenly in Massachusetts on Monday, August 15, soon after conducting the wedding of his daughter Penelope.*

Should she say that? It's true, but it makes her heart hurt.

He was senior minister at the Norwich Congregational Church, where he has served since 1951.

Is that the right year? She'll have to ask her mother. It's too hard to write this now. She takes some deep breaths and then, hoping to calm herself, she picks up Kate's diaries. She skips ahead until an entry stops her.

<u>November 21, 1940:</u> Mother died this afternoon. She has been slipping downhill very rapidly during the last month or so—she said she thought her liver had ceased functioning, and she certainly appeared jaundiced to me—and then this afternoon, while I was sitting with her, she drifted quietly and peacefully into death. Ever a lady, even in dying, she raised no fuss; there were no disturbing death throes. Quite suddenly she was simply gone.

I am grateful that I knew she was dying; in the past few weeks we have spent so many happy hours together remembering the past. I believe that she had grown weary of life—she was ready to leave—and I have no regrets about the manner of her passing, but with her last breath, a crushing weight of sorrow descended upon my heart. Already I miss Mother so much that I can scarcely bear to think of tomorrow and all the rest of my days without her.

What is she going to do about this pregnancy? What would her father tell her to do? If he really wanted grandchildren, should she keep this pregnancy? *Am I ready for that?* Her mother had regrets. *Of going ahead with me.*

At eight o'clock, she takes a seat on the chair next to the only telephone in the Lodge and dials her home number. Listens to the rings. Martin picks up after the fourth one.

"Dad died." She can hear that she sounds angry, perhaps because if Martin had had his way, she wouldn't have been able to squeeze her father's hand for the last time.

"Another heart attack?"

"Yes."

"I'm sorry, Cassie."

"We are holding a memorial service this weekend. Saturday, 2:00 p.m., at Dad's church in Norwich. I hope you can come."

"Of course, sweetie." He sounds so matter-of-fact, she wonders whether she caught him while he was working on his case.

"Thank you, Martin. I'm glad you'll be there." When Martin doesn't say anything more, she concludes, "I'll stop interrupting you. I can tell you're busy. I'll call back tomorrow night."

Feeling terribly alone, she phones Helen with the news.

Helen cries, "Oh, Cassie, no, I'm so sorry. When your father collapsed, I had such a bad feeling."

"I can't believe he's gone."

"How can I help?" Helen asks.

"There's really nothing you can do, but thanks for asking."

Then Cassie calls Aunt Charlotte, asks to come see her again in the morning. Maybe Aunt Charlotte can help her see what to do.

Cassie heads out the door and passes by the lily pond, where the frogs are croaking loudly. She starts up the hill, hoping to find Christopher at home. The scent from shrubs of bay spices the air. As the wake from passing boats rocks the bell buoy, its tolling sounds mournful. Once she reaches the top, she looks out at the scene below. There aren't many lights on at this hour. She hurries toward Christopher's house. As soon as he opens the door to her, she says, "Dad died this morning."

"Oh no." He holds out his arms. She walks into his embrace.

She stands still for a long time, savoring the comfort. Finally, she steps back. "Thank you, Chris. That's exactly what I needed."

"Come in, Cassie. Let me get you a drink."

"I can't sit. I need to move. Come down to the beach with me?"

"Sure. Whatever you want."

Christopher leads her down a narrow trail through the trees; branches brush against them. She'd forgotten about this shortcut. Once the way becomes steep, he reaches back for her hand.

When they reach the beach, she takes off her sandals and starts wading into the ocean. Christopher quickly hitches up his jeans before following her in.

Christopher says, "I love the way the moon lights up a path across the water."

"Granite Cove is so quiet and peaceful tonight." She stirs the water to agitate the algae. "Lots of phosphorescence."

Slapping the water with his palm, Christopher creates little bursts of golden light.

He moves toward Cassie.

"Your father was one of my favorite people. When I thought about going to Alaska after college, my parents didn't like the idea, but your father encouraged me."

"I didn't know that."

"He told me, 'Now's the best time of life to explore and grow up a little more, see what options appeal to you.'"

"Remember how Dad would take a bunch of us kids up to the Little Red Store after dinner so we could get candy?"

"Yes! He gave us each a dollar to spend on whatever we wanted."

"Dad had a sweet tooth too. He probably bought himself some candy, but I never noticed because I was thinking about what I could get."

Christopher steps closer. "Remember the time he loaned me his car to drive us to the winter dance at Norwich Academy?"

"Yes, and it ran out of gas on our way home. He was so embarrassed!" She laughs. Then, a little nervous about how near he is, she retreats. Dipping her hand into the water, she throws some at him.

He tosses water back at her.

Splashing and laughing in the dark, then slowly, like a couple dancing a pavane, they move together. They clasp hands. "CayCay, I—"

"No, don't say anything. I should go."

Back at the Lodge, she scurries around getting ready for bed. She's so stirred up by the feelings Christopher aroused that she hardly knows what to do with herself. As she walks back and forth down the long hall, she acknowledges that she still loves him. She never quite understood why he broke up with her right before he left for Berkeley. He said it was too hard to maintain a long-distance relationship. She'd gone along with him—it would be good for them to spend time apart. She has really missed being with a man who is so warm, who understands and appreciates her.

She goes down to the kitchen to make some chamomile tea in hopes that it will help her sleep. When she returns to bed, she picks up Kate's diaries.

May 24, 1917: The Supreme Court of Massachusetts upheld Van Kleek Allison's conviction on the grounds that he is not a physician and his distribution of the pamphlets was "entirely indiscriminate."

In rendering his opinion, Chief Justice Rugg said, "Manifestly," these statutes "are designed to protect the public morals . . . Their plain purpose is to protect purity, to preserve chastity, to encourage continence and self-restraint, to defend the sanctity of the home, and thus to engender in the State and nation a virile and virtuous race of men and women. The subject matter is well within the most obvious and necessary branches of the police power of the State."

Mr. Allison was sentenced to three years.

Forbidding birth control information is well within "the *police* power of the State"! Wait until Ann hears about this!

October 30, 1917: After numerous arrests for picketing in front of the White House, Alice Paul, leader of the National Woman's Party, started serving a seven-month sentence in the District of Columbia Jail. Then she went on a hunger strike protesting the bug-infested food and hard conditions in the jail. In response doctors have been force-feeding her raw eggs twice a day with a tube down her throat, a process that causes her to vomit repeatedly.

Cassie starts to gag too. She sits up even straighter and breathes deeply.

<u>May 8, 1919:</u> I proposed to the executive committee that we engage an organizer to go into the field and rouse support for the Birth Control League, but the committee voted instead to reorganize under the name Family Welfare Foundation in hopes of enlisting more members—I was the sole dissenter.

I believe the new name is a sign of woeful timidity; it suggests that we are backing down from a struggle that has proven rather difficult. We need more vigor, not less, if we are to succeed in the cause that is most vital to women's health and happiness and thus to the strength of their children.

<u>February 2, 1920:</u> We are closing up the affairs of the Family Welfare Foundation and settling all of our outstanding obligations. These past months have been extremely discouraging, for the programs have roused little interest; attendance at meetings and contributions have fallen off. Doctors Southard, Konikow, Swift, and others will give contraceptive advice to their patients under the rules we formulated, but that seems to be all that is possible at this time. I feel greatly discouraged, but I must admit that I will not miss the frustration of attempting to break through the wall of public indifference.

Now I shall have more time to paint. And since Del bought us land in Wellesley, we have both been preoccupied with planning our new home.

<u>March 13, 1920:</u> Del was asked to write some articles about ferns for Bailey's *Cyclopedia of Horticulture*, and I have been busy illustrating them for him. I seem to have mastered this art of botanical illustration fairly well now, for the work doesn't take me nearly as long as it used to, and Del is pleased with my results.

<u>August 26, 1920:</u> Hallelujah! At long last, women have finally won the right to vote. And now, like the intrepid pioneers of the movement for suffrage, we must forge ahead, courageous and strong as we demonstrate how very well we will use our new right to improve conditions for women and families. We shall employ the franchise to further progress, to combat the bastions of ignorance, and to ensure peace henceforth. Although there will be challenges ahead, it is up to us now to carry the torch of our foremothers, whose sacrifices shall not have been made in vain.

The tide has finally turned. I wonder, if I were to launch a new and more vigorous sort of birth control organization, would it be more likely to succeed now?

<u>September 30, 1920:</u> The first killing frost last night has withered the most fragile flowers and vegetables in the neighborhood, but the heartier species still appeared vigorous when I took my morning walk, kicking through piles of leaves. As I breathed in the deliciously fresh air, I began to feel a sharpening of my appetite for some serious work of my own.

My comrades from the Birth Control League do not believe the time is right yet for a new birth control organization, but there must be something I can do to advance the cause on my own. There is nothing to which I am more deeply committed.

These lawmakers and judges, these churchmen and politicians, do not consider the mothers or the children; they think only of themselves. Their laws defining birth control as obscenity are wholly masculinist, and they are based on a male system of values, where the act of conception is deemed to be more significant than any of its consequences. I suspect that these laws are based on an unspoken attitude about the holiness of intercourse, and the lawmakers, mounting the argument that it is sacrilege to tamper with the holy, have made illegal anything that might interfere with male pleasure.

While I confess that there are, indubitably, occasions upon which intercourse can become a sort of holy experience— times when the nuptial couch is mysteriously transformed into an altar for the communion of two spirits—that is not always the case, and it certainly is not true by definition.

Cassie drops the pages on the bed. Would making love with Christopher be a holy experience? But how can she even ask a question like that right now? She's married to someone else, pregnant, and reeling from the loss of her father.

The breeze picks up. She watches the long white nylon sheers on the sides of the windows blow into the room, dancing like ghosts. She's all alone. There's no one she can tell the whole story to about what she's going through now. No one except maybe Aunt Charlotte.

What the hell is she going to do?

CHAPTER 13

"Hello! Aunt Charlotte?"

"Come in, Cassie!"

As soon as Cassie opens the door, Charlotte puts her hand on Cassie's arm. "I'm so very sorry to hear about your father."

"I can hardly believe he's gone. It doesn't seem real yet."

"Let's talk out on the porch. May I get you some coffee?"

"No, thanks. Maybe a small glass of water, though."

Soon they sit facing each other. "Your mother must be devastated."

"She's coping. Mother's really strong."

"Of course she is. She's a Reed woman."

"Mother doesn't let anything stop her." *Except getting pregnant with me—I stopped her from getting on with her career. But I don't have to follow in her footsteps.*

"Is there something I can do to help?"

"I don't know, Aunt Charlotte. I'm overwhelmed by it all."

"That's understandable," Charlotte says, giving Cassie a small smile.

"How are you doing, Aunt Charlotte? Are you here for the whole summer?"

"I'm fine. I'll leave after Labor Day." She leans forward. "You told me you've been reading Aunt Kate's diaries. What can I tell you about her?"

"Did she talk to you about her abortion?"

"She didn't say much."

"There are no diaries for 1910 and 1911."

"Aunt Kate and her Aunt Sally took the RMS *Mauretania* to France in the fall of 1910. If she wrote in her diary in France, I would not be surprised if she destroyed those writings later. She did tell me the abortionist didn't completely remove the placenta. When infection set in, Aunt Sally got Aunt Kate to a physician, who performed a dilation and curettage."

"That's scraping the inside of the uterus?"

"Right."

"I see." Cassie takes a sip of water. Right now, she doesn't want to think too closely about what that procedure might feel like.

"That botched abortion changed the course of Aunt Kate's life."

"Yesterday my mother told me she got pregnant with me before she and my father were married."

"Your mother is a passionate woman."

"I don't think of her that way."

"Of course you don't—she's your mother."

"The thing is, I'm not so sure about myself. I don't have much passion for my husband. In fact, I'm not sure I want to stay married to him."

Charlotte reaches out and squeezes Cassie's hand.

"And now I know that I definitely am pregnant."

"That complicates things."

"I don't know what to do. Penny is pregnant too. Did you know that?"

"I did wonder why her wedding was arranged so quickly."

"Do you have any advice for me, Aunt Charlotte?"

"This is your life. These are your choices to make, your consequences to bear."

"That's true. I'm the one who'll pay the price for whatever I decide."

"What does your husband say?"

"I haven't told him." The question irritates Cassie. She expected more of Aunt Charlotte. "I don't want Martin to know until I have a better idea of my own feelings," she clarifies.

"I can't tell you what you should do, Cassie."

Cassie's head drops, and her shoulders slump. She clasps her hands tightly together in her lap, trying not to cry. She'd had so much hope that Aunt Charlotte would be able to point out the way to her. Now she feels really discouraged.

Speaking gently, Charlotte says, "You must be drowning in grief."

"I can't think about that yet. I have to write Dad's obituary. My mother claims she's no good at things like that."

Charlotte nods.

"I'd better get back to my draft."

"I wonder, Cassie, would you be interested in seeing some letters of Aunt Kate's? I found them when I moved in here, shoved against the back of a drawer in her desk. They must have been overlooked when the drawer was emptied; I purchased the furniture as well as the house itself."

"You kept them? Why didn't you send them to Smith, so they could be added to the rest of the collection?"

"They're too private."

"I would like to see them—thank you."

"I'll take a look for them this afternoon."

"What's in them?"

"You'll want to see for yourself."

Back at the Lodge, Cassie finds her mother moving all of the wrapped wedding presents onto the porch.

"Load these into the cars, Cassie. I just spoke with Penny. She and

Stephen will take their gifts home after the memorial service. They can have Paul's car too."

"Mom, when you found out you were pregnant with me, what options did you consider?"

"I was very sick during the first few months—"

"Were you tempted to abort?"

"It was too dangerous."

"What would you do in the same situation today? You could get a legal abortion. Would you—"

"I have no idea, Cassie. I can't think about hypotheticals. In fact, I can hardly think at all. Help me load these gifts."

"Mom . . ." She needs time alone. She can't be running every errand Liz thinks of. She has to figure out what she's going to do. If she could get away by herself for a few days . . . "May I take Dad's car?"

"You already have a car in Minnesota, Cassie."

"I just want to take it to Northampton for a few days," she replies. "I'd like to do more research. Then I'll head down to Norwich."

"Now? You want to leave and do research *now*?"

"While I'm still here in the east, I might as well do more work at Smith."

Liz sighs. "Fine. But take the gifts with you. And find some tarps to cover the loot so no one's tempted to steal it."

Cassie says, "I need to finish Dad's obituary. I've drafted it, but I need your input now."

They sit down over cups of coffee. Her mother tells Cassie to take out the part about Paul's dying right after Penny's wedding—it's too personal to put in the newspaper.

After they complete the obit, they sit back and light up their cigarettes. When the telephone rings, it startles them both.

Cassie runs to answer it. Charlotte has found the letters.

Cassie loads her bags into her dad's car and drives over to the Studio.

Charlotte emerges holding a packet of white envelopes wrapped in a red satin ribbon and hands it to Cassie, saying, "I'd like these back eventually."

"I promise to return them."

"How's your mother holding up?"

"She's busy managing everything."

"Her loss won't really hit her until later."

"I'll be in touch, Aunt Charlotte. Thank you."

Once Cassie reaches Route 128 heading west, her mood starts to lift. Driving gets her thoughts moving along with the miles. She doesn't have to follow her mother's path, allowing her life to be derailed by an unexpected pregnancy. She has a choice. There are many decision points that shape the direction your life takes. Some change you forever.

In Northampton, she checks into a motel and eats a quick dinner. She calls her mother, then she pulls the first letter out of its envelope. The paper is thick and cream colored. The tip of the pen must have been very fine, for the words are as thin as spider legs.

Lowell
Oct. 1, 1917

My dear Del:

From our parting, from the absence of letters, I know that you are offended, put out, or indifferent, whatever you may wish to call it—with me and my actions. I feel you are most unjustifiably so and that if either of us is going to make his or her displeasure felt, the privilege is surely not yours.

Will you please hear my case, and may I ask that if this reaches you at the dining table or when you are absorbed in work at the Herbarium, you fold it up and put it away until you can give me your undivided attention?

We were agreed that my sister's children had better leave the Newton house, were we not? I had already told you what I thought I should do in case Lucia's illness became serious, and then when the doctor told me at two o'clock that she had a serious attack of pneumonia, I went straight to you. I told you about it, I asked your advice, I appealed to you for help. In that emergency, however, you did not take the trouble to put down your Herbarium sheet and glass, but with one eye screwed up and the other on the dried fern you answered me in scarcely more than monosyllables. Ashamed that your mother or anyone else should see me begging your attention and receiving scant civility, I left the room—prepared to bear the full burden of the decision and the responsibility of taking the two babies and a new nurse with whom neither was familiar all the way to Lowell that stormy afternoon.

I do not think any judge would say that I am finicky about the small politenesses of life from you. The little attentions that men pay women are always acceptable, but I have passed them by, feeling sure that in a crisis you would show up considerate and helpful. However, those few moments in the library showed me that I could expect no aid.

I shall not dwell on that. In the midst of my preparations, you came in—having realized perhaps by my departure that something was going to happen—and suggested that I take the children over to your brother's. I knew at once that I did not want to, and that if I did go, the whole time I was there would be disagreeable. It is unnecessary to state all the reasons because I told you then and because I do not think they have much to do with the case.

I *preferred* to come here, and because I did you became

angry. Why I cannot imagine. If I had to go away, why should I not go where it was pleasantest, and when you saw that I did not care to take your suggestion, was that any reason for becoming angry? Should you not then have helped me to the best of your ability? Would not any man who felt any care or love for his wife have helped her? You however told me to go where I liked for all you cared—and went off downstairs without a thought as to whether I had money or needed any encouragement or assistance.

And I came alone. God knows how tired I was when I reached here at six o'clock. Baby Mark would not go to his new nurse, and Lucia had to hold my hand, and so we traipsed back and forth in the stations, my back aching so with the weight of Mark that I could have screamed. I say any man of my acquaintance would have left his work to help me, and you—from whom I should expect aid—deserted me entirely. And, moreover, consider that you have a grievance against *me*.

I find that marriage has added to my burdens and has given me none of the personal care and attention that would make these burdens easier to bear. When the baby's weight bore heavily on my back, I resented the fact that I had to bear it alone and that you did not even care.

What I have written may be untactful; it may cause you pain. But I was determined that you should know what my position in this matter is. If, with my feelings outraged, and sick at heart and soul, I can think of you with love and forgiveness and am willing to let the past die, for I still have faith that the good and lovableness in you surpasses the cantankerousness and thoughtlessness, surely any resentment on your part against me because I would not do as you suggested must be dead long ago—that is if your love for me is half as great as mine for you, and you have many times sworn that it was greater.

So, dearest, I hope to hear from you and let me know your side of this unfortunate affair, and then let us both put it away into the farthest recess of our minds and seal the lid.

Lovingly, Kate

This is unsettling. While Cassie is struck by Kate's eloquence, her remarks are all too reminiscent of arguments she and Martin have been having. Marriage can be so difficult. In the past, Cassie would have gone to her father for advice or at least the solace of being listened to.

CHAPTER 14

Northampton, Massachusetts

In the library, which is wonderfully quiet, Cassie calls up box after box from the Kate Easton Papers in the Sophia Smith Collection. She finds diaries from Kate's teenage years through 1909, but then nothing more until 1912, and then the volumes continue uninterrupted until 1960. Charlotte must be right when she guessed that Kate destroyed the volumes from 1910 and 1911.

There are large folders containing the cartoons she read about. Seeing the originals is thrilling. She'll definitely want good copies of these. Then she finds dozens of India ink drawings of ferns, as well as sketchbooks Kate was obviously using to practice drawing human eyes: open and closed, depicted from various angles. On other pages, noses and hands. Then she comes upon additional sketches of the naked woman on the cross, though there aren't any men watching her here. Did Kate ever render her crucifixion in paint, or was she expressing frustration at the way men treat women, or . . . what? If Cassie wants to discover more about this, would she find information about Kate's thinking in her diaries or letters? Or in the box labeled *Art Journals*? She'll have to call for that box.

When she digs into the files of correspondence, she finds letters between Kate and her sister Evelyn, letters from Kate's mother, and ones from her brother, Nat. She skims them quickly and flags several to be copied.

The quantity of material is overwhelming; boxes titled *Genealogy, Financial Records, Real Estate, Newspaper Clippings,* and *Miscellaneous Memorabilia.* There's no way she'll be able to review everything she might want xeroxed. She needs to figure out what to focus on. The box labeled *One Aurora Place* might be worth looking into because its title is so specific.

Another box contains pages and pages of charts showing swatches of color, each shade subtly different from the ones surrounding it. They've all been numbered. And then there's a sketch of a girl wearing a hat with notations of numbers all over her face and dress—Kate must have been noting the colors to use when making a painting based on this pencil sketch.

Cassie opens a folder of photographs. A photo of Kate by the Chickering Studio taken in 1910 shows her to be a lovely young woman with wavy dark hair pinned up in the back to reveal a long white neck, wearing a fancy gown with short puffed sleeves and flowers sewn onto the bodice. Unsmiling, she looks very serious and contained. There's a photo of a stunning portrait of Kate painted by Edmund Tarbell in 1913. And then Cassie comes upon several photos of a naked woman whose arms are loosely tied to a rough wooden cross. This is Kate's model for the crucifixion.

In the box called *Art Journals,* Cassie pages through the notebooks until she finds another sketch of the woman on the cross. Below it, Kate has written, "A series of large wall decorations representing injustices imposed on women by tradition, superstition, the church, the law, the state, marriage and the laws of childbearing, disenfranchisement, inadequate wage, war, etc. *The Crucifixion of Woman* will be the central panel. The nails on the cross will symbolize the church, the state, the law, and the home. The woman will be represented as pregnant, with every mark of marriage taken from different customs and nationalities, such as wedding rings, tattoo marks, hair styles, etc."

If Kate actually painted *The Crucifixion of Woman*, where is it?

Cassie dives into another box of correspondence, but these letters are mundane recitals of weather and health and visits. By 4:00 p.m. she collects copies and leaves the library.

As she climbs into her father's car, she smells his Old Spice and cigarettes, and before grief catches her it is comforting—as if he is with her.

Back at the hotel, she opens the next envelope in the packet from Charlotte.

Newton
October 3, 1917

My dear Kathryn:

This is Monday morning, and I have your letter written on Saturday. I was not in the laboratory when it came, nor anywhere else that would interfere with a continuous and careful reading of your letter. What you have said I cannot repeat word for word, but I have the essence of your thoughts pretty much at command. What you say of me is not surprising; that I fit the picture you paint and perhaps spread beyond the outline drawn to hold in my sinful character is no more than a calm retrospect would lead me to expect.

At least it is gratifying to learn in the end that in spite of all my brutalities, you love me as you did in the beginning. It is, indeed, heartrending to read your complaints because they are of a nature which quite offsets my supposed injuries. I surely do not suffer great discomforts through you, nor do your failings bring about much bodily suffering for me. Your shortcomings are of the exasperating kind that makes a man wonder whether the new woman is such a desirable social adjunct as she is inclined to consider herself.

And yet. I do not care much how you keep house or utilize your time as my grievances are, as I have said, of the nature of exasperation.

You hold up your exodus as a necessary one. Your reasons for it have no foundation in fact. Perhaps for me it would have been well if I had hurried off with you to save you the burden of Mark and to make the journey an easy one, if not enjoyable. But to me what you did revealed the one great trend of your thought: to return to that real home, in which I form no part.

Day by day of late I have seen the desire for something work upon you and in spite of my earnest hope that you would soon settle down and find a home here. You seemed like one with no ambition and in every way homesick. Why should we thrash this thing out anymore? If I am the brute that you have painted, why should you even hope to come to me again while I have greater power than you and can move beyond your reach? Do you think that I want to make you suffer? My real want is to free you from such an unhappy union, to give you back your home, and all your freedom. If I am the inconsiderate thing you have thought me, at least learn that I have sufficient consideration to deny to you absolutely the presence of my faulty body.

Take what you want of mine, what you need, and make your home in Lowell now, rather than wait until I have no need of any home here. Go to your mother, your sisters and brothers, and forfeit the lair of an inconsiderate cad, whose lack of manners makes him a useless husband. Why wait until too late to go home?

Have I laid myself open to your blame, to your condemnation? Why, I blame you, and condemn the things that you do. What a hopeless combination.

Did one eye screw up? May God grant that you never see that eye again.

Yours sincerely,

Del Easton

Del's letter is so cold it makes Cassie feel sick with anxiety. Does she feel upset because this is likely the way Martin would react if she asked for a separation?

Lowell

October 5, 1917

My dear Del,

It is hard to answer your letter, not because there is not a great deal to say, but because I hate to hark back over the miserable business.

The reiteration of your jealousy of my affection for my family does not surprise me, for I know how ineradicable your feeling is, though equally unjustifiable.

The grief of my life is that what I do or leave undone is so excruciatingly irritating to you that it outweighs your love for me. For example, your exasperation was so much greater than any other feeling at the hour of parting that you had no loving thoughts for me.

It is my great misfortune that I arouse your dislike, and such a misfortune is not thrown off with a change of abode. If you could have looked in upon me here you might have felt perfectly satisfied with the punishment I was receiving. I have been miserable, and though I have made an effort that the family should not suspect what my trouble was and have made my cold an excuse for morbid manners, the real truth lies much deeper.

You tell me to go to Mother, to my sisters and brothers, but here I am, and that is not what can make my happiness. Can I never make you believe that? Will you never understand that you—foremost of any in the world—make or mar my existence? And so, from your jealousy of my family I pass to your other proposition of giving me my freedom. Nothing could be further from causing my happiness than such a thing. Nothing could cause me greater grief than the knowledge that you could let me go, or wish your own freedom, exasperating though I am.

As I look back over the last month in Newton, I can see that you are right about the homesickness. And I can also find a thousand excuses for myself, which might be accepted by an impartial judge, but which I know would not satisfy my inmost conscience. For if I had realized the difference it might have made to us both, I could have surmounted the difficulties. Somehow when I got back from Granite Cove at the end of the summer, I felt like loafing, like enjoying the luxuriance about me, and I did. And then I ran the automobile some, and then I tried to get to work, and when I looked about the house, I felt I ought to be at work, and when at work I felt I should be doing something else. But I admit such things are no barriers really, and I might really have done very differently.

But that I did not do such things was no indication that I wished to come here. I had no thought of coming here, except for a day perhaps to see Mother while all the others were away, but then when Evelyn left her children with us for a few days, and Eliza became ill, and I feared for the health of those children for whom I was temporarily responsible— but you already know all about that.

Dear Del, you should not have felt hurt because I spoke of your screwing up your eye—that did not "rile" me—one of

the aspects of my liking for you is that I love your manner-
isms, the quick precise way you use your hands, your clear
way of looking out—even your squint over the microscope.

In proportion to the size of my love is the extent of the
hurt, and you must admit, as indeed you do in your letter,
that I was not unjustified in feeling grieved. But I repeat
again my love rises far beyond such things, and though I
would rather they did not happen, the whole fabric of my
affection is not torn and ruined by them.

With you I see it is harder. My personal peculiarities are
of the nature to make you squirm and to exasperate you.
They overwhelm your love, and it is just here that my great
worry lies.

If I felt that your affection was as strong, as forgiving and
enduring as mine, I should be certain that life would work
out serenely for us both.

And now I am back again to your suggestion of separation. In view of your interpretation of facts, you show great
consideration, but how can your love contemplate such a
thing? How can you cold-bloodedly write it, how can you
seriously consider it? *It is too terrible!*

I have finished the *Jamesonia glutinosa* and almost
completed *Oleandra costaricensis*—both I shall send to you
today—and the sooner they can be reproduced the better, for
I have had to spend a long time on each.

The smooth paper has come from Boston, and I shall
endeavor to carry on the other drawings.

Last evening for the first time since my arrival I have felt
life enough to go out.

Now I am going to work.

Lovingly,

Kate

Newton
October 6, 1917

My dear Kate:

Let alone what has passed and give it no further thought. For me it has been far from pleasurable to gloom over undesired prospects, and if any great good has come out of this anxious period, at least every sheet in my Herbarium has been stamped and numbered, up to six thousand, because my mental machinery has been deeply disturbed. One can do work with the hands when the mind is sick.

Today I worked on the *Fern Icones,* and although my physical condition is not what it was a week ago, I have started well and have hopes of success. Houghton Mifflin & Co. will do all the press work, so with your cooperation the first fascicle ought to go through seasonably.

Nothing has happened here of much account, and I keep mostly by myself. Last night I ran the numbering machine until my arms and nerves ached. Otherwise my hours have been dull.

I have cabled an offer to Mrs. Lehmann and now await a letter from her that may get here in four weeks or more. I hope to get the Herbarium, and Dr. Robins says I ought to have no difficulty in selling the non-fern specimens.

I feel, unjustifiably or not, that the *Fern Icones* provides an outlet for my best achievement, a knowledge of ferns, directly through such a publication, whether it proves profitable financially or not.

Furthermore, it calls for your cooperation, and with your skill added to my persistency, *Fern Icones* ought to take rank as the best thing of its kind that ever left the press.

If happiness is the one end for which we should strive,

what greater happiness can be conceived than a man and a woman who have chosen to breast the world together working mutually to inform themselves and to contribute to the knowledge of mankind? If you could enjoy it as I do, even if the labor required on your part consumed but two hours a day, the end gained would be an ample dividend for the effort.

You speak of courtesies men show to women, of the kindly relations of married lives which you judge of only from public display and know nothing of as they progress behind closed doors. Did you ever consider the envy not of women alone, but of men, who see tangible results of the community of interest in the pursuits of married people? Here you and I have an opportunity to work together. I am naturally the more enthusiastic because in me is vested the greater ambition to achieve the end. Isn't it to be in cooperative work that the best we can do together is to be done, and isn't it well for us to follow the present road until advancing years show us a road that can prove more elevating and more useful if followed by people of taste and ability?

I fear you follow me half-heartedly, not enthusiastically, but let me assure you I realize well that ships were not devised to sail on dry land nor houses to float on water. Each one to his taste, and if you and I must suffer the agony of bewailing each other's tastes, we only have ourselves to blame. And so, with advancing night, I'll say simply,

Forget it!

DE

Cassie is amazed to realize that Kate and Del separated for a time. They probably would have divorced if Kate hadn't been so clear about her unhappiness at that prospect. She hung on to her husband with all her might while at the same time expressing her feelings about his unhelpful behavior.

But Del annoys Cassie. Although he has moved on from their quarrel, he's condescending to Kate as an artist while at the same time trying to manipulate her into becoming his illustrator and embracing his work as her own. Was Kate busy drawing suffrage cartoons when Del wrote this letter? Cassie flips back through the pages of Kate's diaries. No, the cartoons came earlier.

CHAPTER 15

SS *Saxonia*
October 14, 1919

My dear little Kate:

Although the weather is fair and the sun is shining, I feel mentally lonely and miserable. The trouble is I want to be with you, and the thought that I am drawing farther and farther away from you instead of approaching you nearer and nearer is a constant source of exasperation and chagrin. I am not exactly suffering from an ordinary attack of the "blues," but no matter how earnestly I try to be stoical and to think, after all, that it is really for a good purpose that I am on my way to England, the love of you comes strongly to me, and I know that it is you, all the time, who order and rule my life and inclinations, and that you only can bring into my days security from homesickness and loneliness.

After lunch the first day out, I had the electrician put drop lights in the staterooms, and now the illumination is far better than that afforded by the one small bulb in the ceiling. Although the others do not seem inclined to work, I pulled out my trunks and settled down to microscopic work. But thoughts of you keep intruding.

Since you have been visiting your sister, you may feel more than ever before that we ought to have a house of our own, and therefore you may regard my desire for more bookcases as an earnest of my intention to remain in the old homestead.

Out here on the sea I realize the hopelessness of one who is unidentified with a birth place, and I dread the idea of leaving behind me family and personal associations, but I am ready to make the move that pure reason dictates, and to abide by the verdict of common sense. Although I have followed a course that I considered the only wise one, I realize, dear one, that my decision to live in the old homestead was not fair to you or kind, and while I may yearn for a permanent residence in the place of my origin, I am quite ready to make amends for an error that I could not foresee.

Heretofore, I have argued selfishly, allowing my own grievances precedence over yours, and when I have considered and reconsidered the situation from my own viewpoint, I have selfishly overlooked your position and thereby rendered myself culpable of a serious offense against our mutual good. To be happy, really happy, we must hold strongly to the belief in equality, and cultivate intensively that mutual ground, with the ambition to establish in our relations a permanent and admirable affection. When one of us continually gives way to the desires of the other, the danger is intensified of losing one's God-given individuality, and I love you too well to brave the crime of demolishing for the sake of my own creature comforts a nature and individuality as noble and kind as I know and feel yours to be.

For you, I must do what is best and wisest, and to make you happy and contented, I am quite ready to give up all that I love in Newton. You gave up your home to come to me. That was an act of bravery for which I admire you. Is it to be said of me that I was unwilling to do what common decency required, namely, give you a home of comfort and freedom? We must consider well what we are to do in the future.

Tonight, I shall indulge in a warm bath and hope for a sound sleep in which I may dream a little of you.

I will write again tomorrow.

Del

No wonder Kate kept leaving Del's house in Newton when trouble arose—she never felt it was her home. Perhaps the *One Aurora Place* box documents their new place. She'll check that out in the morning. Kate refers to her mother-in-law as "Mrs. Easton" or "Del's mother." Does that suggest that she doesn't like her, or is it simply that modes of address were more formal in those days? In any case, it's clear that Kate and Mrs. Easton were not close.

Wellesley
August 10, 1947

My dear Kate:

This morning my pen gave out. The mechanism suddenly dried, and the ink gushed out over a new supply of cards. So, I went to Boston to have repairs made and was at work again at one thirty.

The band gave a concert last night in mist. We have had a few drops of rain today. As a result of all this dampness, the front door is firmly shut, and my customary exit is by the library middle window.

I have one other topic to consider. I will open it by saying that modern civilization seems to me to be in danger of scoring a touchback. That is of scoring for the devil behind its own goal line. I saw a picture in a magazine last night that showed a so-called bathing breakfast. Four or five women seated at coffee after a morning dip in the swimming pool. This picture showed anatomy in the "three strikes and out" sense. Rolled-down stocking tops, bare knees, inadequate covering. The stockings might have been taken from one of those pornographic photographs that are sometimes smuggled through the Customs House. The point is that the world progressed from nakedness from other causes besides temperature, and that in this modern freedom in terms of exposure, we are going back to questionable times. From riding sidesaddle to riding astride for women is progress. To begin to accentuate sex by inordinate exposure of extremities is a retrograde tendency. I am no prude, as you know. I am quite liberal in my views. I am anxious that women should adopt a type of clothing that will give as much freedom as men obtain from their clothing. But I am not anxious to have the sexual character of the female of the species on parade.

Well—that is off my mind, and I am going to walk out and see if there is any blue overhead.

Always faithfully yours,

Del

The following day, Cassie glances at the *One Aurora Place* box. It contains blueprints, invoices, and other material documenting construction of Kate and Del's new home in Wellesley. Then she focuses on the records of the Family Welfare Foundation, the Birth Control League of Massachusetts, and the New England Women's Hospital. In the correspondence, she finds a four-page single-spaced letter Kate wrote to Margaret Sanger dated June 29, 1934, in which Kate argues that Sanger's proposed amendment to the U.S. Penal Code doesn't go far enough. Kate closes with the statement, "I am sending under separate cover some occlusive pessaries made from condoms and rings and a rough sketch on how to roll them that I hope will be of interest to you."

Cassie is not surprised to learn that Kate knew Margaret Sanger, but she's amazed that Kate would argue with Sanger. She must have been very sure of herself. Unfortunately, the occlusive pessaries sent under separate cover do not appear in the box with this letter. Cassie would have liked to see what they looked like.

She picks up another letter, written by Kate to her sister.

> Start with a darning ring, the sort made for mending socks—not an embroidery ring, which is not flexible enough. I buy half-gallon cans of Latex in liquid form, one can each of blue, green, pink, and yellow. The Latex hardens on contact with air, so I dip each ring in the latex and hang it up to dry on strings. Each size of ring has its own color. I will do anything necessary to provide women with choice about becoming pregnant or not, whether it is legal or not. I hate the Catholic Church with a passion because of its enslavement of women.

Wow. She had never thought about the contraceptive devices women must have cooked up when birth control was illegal. *Way to go, Kate.* How would she get these homemade diaphragms to the women who needed them?

The day flies by as Cassie digs through folders, marking typescript speeches on birth control and on portrait painting to be copied. She notes an article entitled "Margaret Sanger's Influence" that Kate wrote in 1958; a typescript titled "History of the Birth Control Movement in Massachusetts," no date; and an article from *Fortune* magazine entitled "The Birth-Control 'Pill'" by Robert Sheehan, published in April 1958.

After Cassie exits with a new stack of papers in her bag, she wanders through the campus, then down the hill along Main Street. The heat is nauseating, and soon her cotton blouse is sticking to her chest and back. The noise of cars honking seems very loud after the hushed atmosphere of the library. She enters the first coffee shop she sees. After ordering an iced tea and a sugar cookie, she sits at a little round table next to the window where she can watch the people walking by. She'd been absorbed all day, but now, suddenly, she feels very tired. She realizes she's been keeping herself busy the way her mother does, but in fact she has not been able to leave her problems behind—they still lurk in the background.

That night, when she opens the rest of the letters Charlotte gave her, she's surprised to find that they have to do with the Birth Control League of Massachusetts. Why aren't these letters part of the collection at Smith?

January 2, 1935

Dear Mrs. Del Easton,

I want to put you en rapport with the latest happenings in the Publicity Committee. I was particularly sorry that you were not there yesterday, for my Committee got so enthusiastic about what they could do that they asked for extra power and responsibility to coordinate and develop the publicity. The power of having charge of all publicity was delegated to them by the Executive Committee *for an experimental period,* to be taken back if they fail.

My Committee is a vigorous group. They *want* to work and are bursting with ideas and have enlisted the services of some professional experts at publicity. I felt as I know you would, that these young people *must* take up the burden of this job, that the rest of us have done the pioneer work and have a right to some relief now.

I feel like giving them their head and seeing what they can do. The immediate necessity is of course the financial emergency, and they want to try taking part of the list of social register people and send a different kind of circular, then see what results that brings before they send out the originally planned material. It is an innocent experiment and might succeed, so they are set to try it.

I talked it over with Mrs. Jones, and she gave some wise advice. Of course, she will be my sheet anchor in holding my wild young committee to the course!

I do not think there is anything we have done of which you would disapprove. I certainly hope not, for your wisdom and experience is unique in this whole matter.

Cordially yours,
Olivia Richardson

The Birth Control League of Massachusetts
3 Joy Street
Boston

Sunday, January 6, 1935

My dear Mrs. Richardson,

As president of the Birth Control League of Massachusetts, I forbid the Publication Committee to publish in newspapers or to send out notices in any form under the name of the Birth Control League of Massachusetts or over my name as president, and if the notice in the *Transcript* of January 5 is to be repeated in that or any other newspaper, it must be countermanded until the Executive Committee meets and takes further action.

The article appearing in the *Transcript* of January 5 starting "Taxpayers!" was not submitted to me as president. It was printed over my name, although you know I had made the strongest protest against such unauthorized and unconstitutional use of my name.

And worst of all, the statement that "Our organization exists to help those parents have only as many children as they can support" is absolutely untrue. The implication that two hundred and fifty thousand women are to be prevented from having children unless they can support them is also untrue; such a program would be cruel and unfair to those families who are on public relief through no fault of their own. We stand for something more than saving money for the taxpayers' pockets, and it is a shame that our first newspaper notice to the general public should be based on such a motive.

You had my verbal objection to the form of advertisement you read to me by telephone on Friday morning. I asked you to go to the lawyer and change the wording so as to avoid the appearance of advocating abortion, because of the unfortunate tendency of some people to confuse birth control with abortion, etc. I had already requested that notices should be presented to me properly written in final form. It never occurred to me that you would disregard all my protests and requests and release your material without submitting it to me in its final form.

As a matter of common courtesy, in view of my visit to you and my endeavor to carry on with you amicably, you should have let me see the material to be printed over my name.

Sincerely yours,
Kathryn Easton

The Birth Control League of Massachusetts
3 Joy Street
Boston

January 6, 1935

Dear Executive Committee member:

I have felt compelled to write the enclosed letter to Mrs. Richardson.

There are such misstatements in the advertisement and so many possible consequences that I am considering the advisability of a formal letter to the editor of the *Transcript* repudiating responsibility for the advertisement itself.

The advertisement in the hands of Father Corrigan, or any opponent of birth control, is a weapon with which we can be attacked again and again. In it, our appeal for support is not based on broad humanitarian motives but is based on the motive of saving money alone. Think of addressing a gathering of voters in a future legislative campaign appealing to their human sympathies, and then being faced by an opponent who waves this advertisement and who accuses the League of camouflaging under pretty talk its printed purpose of saving the taxpayers money—for which purpose the advertisement says our organization exists.

Besides it is false from beginning to end. For example,

(1) The total number of births, rich and poor, dead and alive, in Massachusetts was 70,868; so, the taxpayers of Massachusetts could not have supported through public relief two hundred and fifty thousand children born last year.

(2) Refer to our constitution and see what our organization exists for!

(3) Preventive work is different from preventive

medicine—it is not even the same as prevention of conception; it implies coercion; it may be interpreted to mean
restriction of birth by abortion, or sterilization. Voluntary
regulation of conception is our idea, isn't it?

Sincerely yours,
Kathryn Easton

Was Kate embarrassed about her dispute with Olivia Richardson—
is that why these letters were hidden in a drawer? She thinks
about Kate's wanting to ensure that the Birth Control League of
Massachusetts was never seen to support abortion. Understandable
given her experience in Paris. She probably assumed that legalizing
birth control would mean that women would never need an abortion.
Of course, it's not that simple, as her own experience proves.

Wondering what happened next with the League, Cassie pulls out
the diaries.

January 31, 1935: During these weeks of unpleasantness
with Mrs. Richardson and the Publicity Committee, I have
undertaken a thorough soul-searching, for I have come to
question whether I have outlived the term of my usefulness
as president of the Birth Control League. I began in this role
nearly twenty years ago. Have I grown too old-fashioned in
my methods to be effective now? I certainly do not wish to
impede progress for our cause.

Since it has become apparent that the younger members of
the group are eager to assume responsibility, I think it may be
for the best if I step aside and make way for new leadership. I
shall find other ways in which I can help to advance the cause.

So, Aunt Kate stepped down. What happened next? Does the
Birth Control League have a relationship to Planned Parenthood?

There's still so much Cassie doesn't know about Kate and the Birth Control League of Massachusetts, but she senses a rich opportunity here. This could be the heart of her dissertation.

And what about *The Crucifixion of Woman*? She can't wait to tell Ann about that. Cassie's mind lurches back and forth between Kate and the choices looming before her. Then she picks up the telephone.

"Chris, it's Cassie."

"Where are you?"

"I'm in Northampton doing research on Aunt Kate, but I'm heading down to Norwich tomorrow."

"How's it going?"

"I'm finding a lot of great stuff. But that's not why I called. Dad's memorial service is on Saturday. It'll be so difficult." Her voice starts to wobble.

"Shall I come? I could provide moral support."

"Would you, Chris? That would be wonderful." If she can observe her husband and Christopher together in the same place at the same time, perhaps that'll help her figure out what she needs to do.

Christopher says, "You know I really liked your father, but I've never been to a memorial service before."

"I think it's pretty much the same as a funeral."

"Okay." He adds, "I was thinking about you last night. There was a crowd of lightning bugs in the yard, and I remembered how much you liked them."

"I'll never forget the time we caught a few and put them in a jar, thinking we could use them instead of a flashlight to find our way in the dark. Their lights went out when they were no longer free to fly around." She stops speaking, struck by the thought that perhaps her feeling that she's no longer free has extinguished her own light.

He says, "We were so young. Maybe ten years old at the time."

"Even younger."

"I still think lightning bugs are kind of magical."

"Me too." She pauses. *Do I have the nerve?* "I have a question, Chris. Why did you break up with me after graduation?"

"I thought we could use some time apart, to see other people, to get a better idea of what we had together. If we were meant to be partners for life, I assumed we'd figure that out and get back together."

"I was so sad and hurt for such a long time."

"I'm sorry, Cassie. I've felt a lot of regret myself."

"Oh." *Does that mean he still cares?* She listens to him breathing on the other end of the line. When he doesn't add anything more, she says, "Well, I shouldn't keep you. See you Saturday."

CHAPTER 16

Norwich, Connecticut

Her parents' white clapboard Colonial looks lonely. The curtains are drawn, and the front door is shut. Inside, she finds her mother on the phone at her desk, a yellow pad covered with writing under her elbow, the ashtray beside her overflowing. With her free hand, Liz waves her in. The house smells stale. Cassie takes her bags up to her old bedroom, then starts opening all the curtains and windows on the second floor.

When she gets to her parents' bedroom, she walks into her father's closet. Surrounded by his things, it feels as though he's embracing her, but he's not—that will never happen again. Grabbing the lapels of one of his suit jackets, she leans forward to inhale his scent in the fabric. Quietly she asks, "What should I do, Dad?"

Downstairs, after Cassie finishes opening windows, she returns to the kitchen as Liz hangs up the phone. "We've got a long list to attack today."

"How are you doing, Mom?"

"Okay, so long as I keep busy. I've asked the women's auxiliary to handle the food after the service."

Suddenly, Cassie feels terribly nauseated. She was fine most of the time in Northampton. The phone rings again. She moves cautiously, pulling a box of saltines out of the pantry. She eats gingerly while Liz tells the caller, "I don't give a damn what they cost! I've got to have birds of paradise for the bouquets in the church. Paul sent me birds of paradise every time I had a baby."

Liz picks up the whiskey bottle that's sitting out on the counter and pours some into a short glass.

Alone with her mother, Cassie is assailed by her father's absence. Her heart hurts.

She moves into her father's study, closes the door behind her, and sits down at the desk where he wrote his sermons. The room smells like old cigarette smoke. She looks at all the little drawers in front of her, pulls out a few. She finds business cards of social workers and therapists and funeral home directors, rolls of stamps, scissors, and tape. The more she thinks about him, the harder she cries.

A while later Cassie hears Nanny arrive. Nanny tells Liz, "Now we're two old widows together."

Cassie wonders, can she bear any more losses herself?

Penny and Stephen arrive, and Penny immediately corners Cassie. "Mom . . . how is she doing?"

"She's her usual busy self."

"What about you, Cassie?"

"I'm definitely pregnant—I know that for sure."

"Aren't you glad?"

"Not really."

"It would be so much fun to have babies together, Cassie! I can just see us with our little kids running around Granite Cove together."

Cassie can imagine it too. She remembers spending endless summer days playing with her cousins and neighbors like Christopher. It was the best part of her childhood, and she'd love to be able to give her own child experiences like that. She's still torn. She really wants to have children eventually.

"I'm thinking about separating from Martin."

"Oh no! That would be such a radical thing to do. Can't you work things out with him? Maybe you should go see a marriage counselor together."

"I don't know how that could possibly help," Cassie says. "Martin's and my values are just too different. That's never going to change."

"You mustn't get divorced! You can't do that to Mother—not now. She'd be so embarrassed and ashamed."

"I can't stay married for Mom's sake."

"Maybe if you could just wait a while."

Cassie sighs.

Penny says, "Where is Martin, anyway?"

"He's going to meet us at the church. He couldn't get away from his office any earlier."

"What time do we need to get over there?"

"Mother wants us there by one to make sure everything's in order."

Penny checks her watch.

Cassie says, "Christopher's coming to the service. I spoke with him last night." *Should I tell Penny how I feel about Christopher?*

"I can't listen to this. You've got to pull yourself together, Cassie!"

"You're right, Penny. One thing at a time. Right now, it's Dad. I've got to finish my remarks for the service."

CHAPTER 17

"I would like to welcome each of you and to thank you all for coming to honor my father today." Cassie grasps the lectern with both hands and takes a deep breath. The church is packed. She can see Martin in the front row. Although they'd been sitting side by side, they hadn't said much to each other. Everyone has recited Psalm 23 in unison, sung "Our God Our Help in Ages Past." They listened to the lessons and sang "Onward Christian Soldiers," and then the memorial remarks began. Her father's best friend said some words, and now it's Cassie's turn. Moved by the size of the crowd, she continues, "My father touched each of us in this room in very special ways. He gave himself to those he cared about, often to the exclusion of himself. My father's love for his family, his sense of responsibility to all the generations that went before and those to come, formed the essence of his soul."

She pauses, looks around the room. "And by family, I mean men and women, of all ages, whose lives were a part of his. People who considered him a father, people who were intimate friends, people whose lives he touched, all of you here and others who can't be here today. One of Dad's most important contributions to the community was to create the Teen Counseling Center, which has provided mental health services to hundreds of troubled teens and their parents over the past fifteen years. Dad didn't toot his own horn. I only learned today about the fact that Dad gave our babysitter Mary Beth an interest-free loan, so she could go to Jerusalem for her junior year abroad. Mary Beth told me that experience changed her life in profound ways.

"Having this extended, embracing family was one of the most special things about my father. He was well loved, for he loved us all so well. He will be sorely missed."

Her eyes land on Christopher. He's sitting near Eleanor White, a good friend of hers from high school. Her heart lifts. "But he would not have us mourn. Today is the celebration of his life, his spirit, his belief in goodness, his love. So, let us march forward now, enriched by having known him, inspired by what we learned from him. Let us celebrate the power of love."

She takes her seat as Penny gets up to say a few words. One other friend of her father's addresses the room, and then the choir sings Mozart's "Ave verum corpus." The music is so gorgeous it causes tears to stream down Cassie's cheeks. Reverend Fisher provides memorial prayers, and the congregation sings "Joyful, Joyful." After the benediction, Reverend Fisher announces the reception will be held in the Founder's Hall.

The guests mingle, children grab cookies and dash through the crowd, and Cassie hugs Penny. "I liked what you had to say, sister."

"You too, Cassie."

"Good." Cassie sees Christopher walking toward her; she's suddenly overcome with embarrassment. Not here, not now. She should *not* be responding to him like this today. "Thank you for coming, Christopher," she tells him.

"He was a good man."

"Cassie!" cries a familiar voice. "It's been years!"

She turns to Eleanor. "Ellie, thank you for coming. How are you?"

"I'm fine. I married! Phil's great and we live nearby. Are you in town for a while?"

Martin appears at her side. She says, "No, we have to fly back to Minnesota tomorrow."

Martin scrutinizes Cassie's face. "You look exhausted," he says.

"Well, call me," Eleanor says. "I'd love to catch up with you." She walks away.

Cassie looks back and forth between Martin and Christopher, both of whom are watching her.

Awkwardly, she asks, "Martin, did you meet Christopher at the wedding last weekend?"

Martin replies coolly, "We met."

He looks preppy in his navy-blue suit, white shirt, and navy tie with white dots on it. She used to think of Martin as an Adonis with dark hair.

"Is that a new tie?" She can't think of anything else to say to him.

"Yes."

Christopher takes a step forward. He looks a little sloppy but comfortable in a dark corduroy jacket, baggy trousers, and a plaid tie she's seen before. "That was a great service, Cassie. The music was glorious, and I thought you captured your father's spirit very well."

She longs to hug him, but with her husband standing there, she simply replies, "Thank you, Christopher." She can't talk to him in front of Martin. She looks down.

Christopher says, "I need to speak with your mother, Cassie. Excuse me."

She smiles apologetically at him. Then she tells Martin, "I should circulate." She cannot stand beside this stiff man any longer.

Once the reception winds down, Cassie and Martin return to the family home with Liz, Nanny, Penny, and Steven. Cassie and Penny warm one of the many casseroles that people had brought over, and then they all move into the dining room.

Penny says, "The flowers were gorgeous, Mom. So many different colors."

"Your father was well regarded," Liz replies, taking a big swig from her glass of whiskey. "I hope someone collected all the notes that accompanied the arrangements."

"We got them," Cassie says, "and we wrote which bouquet each card went with."

"Thanks, girls."

"A telegram arrived from Matt a little while ago," says Penny. "He expects to get here by the first of September."

Liz's lower lip starts to tremble.

"Thank you for giving us Father's car," Penny adds. "We can really use it."

Liz nods.

Nanny says, "You should eat something, Lizzie."

Cassie remembers her mother saying the same thing to Nanny not that long ago, though it feels like an age. She can barely force herself to eat either, but she has learned that eating seems to keep the nausea at bay.

When Liz rises, Cassie gets up too. She puts her arms around her mother and holds on tight. It feels really good to hug her, even though her breasts are awfully sore. "I'm so sorry, Mummy. I don't know what we're going to do without him."

"I have no idea," Liz replies.

The family disperses to their rooms soon thereafter.

Martin shuts the door of Cassie's bedroom and faces her. "It was so quiet at home last week I could hardly bear it. I missed you, Cassie."

Still standing, she says, "There's something I have to tell you, Martin." She inhales deeply and then exhales. "I'm pregnant."

The look on his face quickly shifts from surprise to pleasure. "That's great news!" He reaches out and takes her hands.

She pulls away. "I don't think I'm ready to become a mother now. I want to be a mom someday, but not yet. I need to get my PhD first."

"What are you saying?"

"I've thought and thought about this. I'm not ready to have a child yet. I have other work I need to complete first."

"Here, sit down. Let's talk about this."

Cassie joins him on the edge of the bed.

"You can keep working on your dissertation. We'll hire a nanny to help you take care of the baby."

"But I'd want to be able to pay attention to a newborn, not be running off to the library all the time."

"Well, what do you want? You want a baby; you don't want a baby. Make up your mind!"

"I have made up my mind. It's my life. This is not the right time for me to have a child. My mother is grieving; my sister is pregnant. They need me now. I want to be available to them."

"It would be great for your mother to have a grandchild to distract her."

"Mom will have Penny's baby."

Martin shakes his head. "You're being unbelievably selfish, Cassie. All you can talk about is yourself. What about me? I want us to start a family—our family!"

I'll be tied to Martin forever if I have this baby. "I'm thinking about getting an abortion."

"You've got to be kidding."

"No, I'm not."

"You're talking about aborting my child—you can't do that! This is my child too. I have rights here."

"Your child? And how would you go about raising *your* child? You spend fourteen hours a day at the office." Now Cassie's furious. "This is not about you. It's my body, my choice. I have the right to choose."

"You've changed, Cassie. Being my wife used to make you happy."

"I *have* changed," she admitted. "I'm no longer willing to lead a life like my mother's."

"You've gotten so independent, I wonder if you even want a husband anymore."

"Sometimes I wonder too."

"You must be a lesbian. That's the only logical explanation."

"No!"

"I tell you, if you have an abortion, there will be serious consequences." Now he sounds nasty.

"That's a threat."

"It's a fact. If you get an abortion, that's the end of our marriage. I'll sue for divorce." His voice is icy cold. "You'd better think very carefully." He stands and moves toward the bathroom.

Once they're in bed, they lie facing away from each other.

Whether to stay with Martin and whether to go through with this pregnancy are two separate issues, but he has wrapped them up together. What if this is my only chance to be pregnant and I'm throwing it away? I do want a child when I'm ready. If I have an abortion, I won't be able to go back on that decision—not ever. It will follow me for the rest of my life.

She slides out from under the covers. Tiptoeing down to her father's study, she sits in his favorite chair.

What is she going to do about her pregnancy? Abortion and divorce or giving up her academic ambitions: each choice is agonizing in its own way.

Cassie keeps going back and forth on this decision.

Her nerves squirm at the prospect of losing the security of her marriage.

What about money? If she and Martin split up, she'll have to get a job.

She can't quite face what she knows in her gut she needs to do.

Her stomach is clenched so hard it feels like it's encased by a blood pressure cuff that's tightening more and more.

But isn't that what it gets down to? What she knows in her gut?

On Monday she'll talk with the people at Planned Parenthood. At least she has the option of choosing a path that will be much safer than the one Kate took. She has no doubt that this will be the hardest thing she's ever done.

CHAPTER 18

Saint Paul, Minnesota

On Monday outside the Planned Parenthood clinic in Highland Park, Cassie makes her way through a crowd of protesters who shout "Baby killer!" and other epithets at her until she gets in through the front door. The guard sitting inside at a desk asks for her name and identification. After he consults a list, he directs her to the waiting room, where eight women are seated, a few of them with men. She checks in with the receptionist and then she waits, thinking about what she's just read about different kinds of abortion described in *Our Bodies, Ourselves* by the Boston Women's Health Book Collective. They are endometrial aspiration, early uterine evacuation, dilation and evacuation, dilation and curettage, and vacuum suction. They all sound scary.

Once she's called into an office, she meets with a nurse, who takes an extensive medical and sexual history and then conducts a complete physical and pelvic exam. She asks about Cassie's blood type and Martin's and how long it's been since her last period. The nurse assures her that the physician will remove her IUD in any case, whether she gets an abortion or not, because the IUD would interfere with the proper development of the fetus. If she wants an abortion, the IUD would be removed after the physician provides her with a paracervical block and dilation. The nurse says since it's only been eight weeks since her last menstrual period, it would be a vacuum suction abortion. She offers a lot of information about what that procedure would actually entail and how to prepare for it. Then she asks what Cassie wants to do for her family planning needs in the future. Cassie says she'll go on the pill, so the nurse gives her a prescription.

Cassie is taken into another office—this time with a counselor whose master of social work degree certificate is mounted on the wall behind her, adjacent to a striking photo of pink, white, and red peonies. Ms. Jones has large glasses, and her blonde hair is tied up in a knot on top of her head. She's wearing a deep purple blouse. As she invites Cassie to sit down, her smile is warm.

Ms. Jones asks, "How are you feeling about your pregnancy, Cassie?"

"I feel like I did something wrong. I *have* an IUD. That was supposed to protect me. I thought I was practicing safe sex. I feel like my body betrayed me."

"It's not fair," Ms. Jones replies, nodding.

"I feel ashamed too. Was I supposed to get a different kind of IUD, one that works better?"

"No, Cassie, you did everything you could. You behaved responsibly."

"I tried." Her voice starts to falter. She doesn't want to cry in front of someone she doesn't know.

Gently Ms. Jones asks, "Are you certain that abortion is the right choice for you?"

"Absolutely. I'm about to start writing the dissertation for my PhD. This is no time for me to have a baby."

"What about the father?"

"We're probably getting divorced." She and Martin were up late last night fighting about her decision. He tried bribing her with a trip to Paris. He said he'd even cut back on his hours at work if that would convince her to have the baby, but nothing he came up with could change what she knows she must do. The sooner she gets this abortion, the better. This morning he told her if she's really going through with it, she should move out.

"I see." Ms. Jones looks intently into Cassie's eyes. "Do you have any fears you'd like to discuss?"

"Will an abortion hurt my chances of a successful pregnancy in the future?"

"No. I've seen many patients with abortions who later had babies."

"That's a relief. I really think I'll want children eventually." Her heart softens at the thought of holding an infant, but then she feels sad—she just has to wait until she can hold her own child.

As she drives over to her friend Ann's apartment with her suitcase, she hangs on to the thought that her unborn fetus does not have more rights than she does. Getting an abortion is simply the most responsible choice she can make at this point in her life.

The next morning, she calls to schedule her abortion. She's told not to eat anything after midnight and to plan to be at the clinic for six hours.

Ann asserts, "If men could get pregnant, abortion would be a sacrament—that's what Gloria Steinem says and I agree." It's Thursday morning and Ann is driving Cassie to the Planned Parenthood clinic on Ford Parkway. "It's crazy that some states are making access to abortion more difficult."

Cassie feels so nauseated she doesn't reply. She's using all her energy to hang on to her stomach so that she doesn't start throwing up in Ann's car.

While Ann sits with a book in the waiting room, Cassie signs in, answers questions, and is given a pregnancy test. After another pelvic exam administered by a nurse, someone draws her blood. She exchanges her clothes for a hospital gown, and eventually she's taken into the procedure room. Frightened now about how much this is going to hurt, she starts to tremble.

Glad to see that the physician is a woman, Cassie asks, "How long will this take?"

"Around fifteen minutes."

Cassie gets up on the table, scoots toward the end, and opens her legs. She steels herself for what is to come.

The doctor explains, "I'm injecting a local anesthetic into the anterior lip of your cervix before I attach the tenaculum."

Cassie says, "Please spare me the details."

"Now try to hold still," the doctor says.

Another woman stands next to Cassie and takes her hand. "I'm Mary. I'll be here with you the whole time, Cassie," she says. "Squeeze my hand as hard as you want. We'll give the anesthetic a couple more minutes to take effect, and then Dr. Schmitt will start."

Dr. Schmitt inserts something like a speculum into her but it's different because it opens up Cassie's vagina wider than it's ever been opened before. That hurts.

Mary starts asking Cassie all sorts of questions about what she's been studying, which helps distract her.

The doctor says, "I'm removing the IUD now."

Cassie feels a brief but strong pull in her uterus. Then it stops.

Dr. Schmitt says, "Wiggle your toes if you're in pain."

Cassie stares at the perforated ceiling tiles, trying not to weep, but hot tears leak down into her ears when the doctor starts to vacuum out her insides. Mary wipes her tears, murmuring, "You're doing fine, Cassie, you'll be all right, you're doing a great job here, you're a brave woman, everything's going to be all right. Hang on now, just a little bit longer."

With the last sweep of the vacuum, Cassie starts cramping below her belly button. She wiggles her toes. The pain increases.

Mary says, "Almost done now, Cassie."

After several more minutes, Dr. Schmitt says, "You can put your legs down."

Cassie is wheeled into the recovery room. She can't stop crying. She's relieved that it's over and she isn't nauseous any longer, but she feels as though her chest and heart and stomach and guts have been thoroughly hollowed out.

An hour later Cassie is warned about what to do if she starts spotting or bleeding too much, and then she's allowed to leave.

Ann drives home. Cassie's eye is caught by how red the sumac is turning. The color of blood. It'll be autumn soon, getting colder and darker.

Cassie spends the rest of the day in bed, sleeping or staring at a poster of Modigliani's *Portrait of a Polish Woman* mounted on the far wall. The woman's neck is curved, her eyes are closed, and her hands are folded in her lap. Cassie wonders what she's thinking. She is so tired. After another long nap, she sits up. She hopes to God she hasn't just made a mistake she'll regret for the rest of her life. When she called Penny last night to tell her what she was going to do, her sister was very sad. She said not to tell their mother—she doesn't need this news right now. Cassie might have called her cousin Helen, but with Helen on the verge of delivering her own baby, that didn't make sense. Ann has been a true friend throughout this ordeal. Maybe Cassie should call Charlotte now—she might be able to provide some comfort. But Cassie feels too wobbly to call Charlotte—she'd probably start sobbing again. Perhaps going back to the diaries will help.

CHAPTER 19

February 19, 1928: Ten days ago, the Boston police arrested Dr. Antoinette Konikow for conducting a lecture and demonstration of contraceptive methods before patients and friends in her office. This evening about twenty of us met at Dr. Konikow's home to hear about her predicament. We voted to revive the Birth Control League and reinstated the former officers. Hallelujah! The time is finally right to take up the torch again.

March 2, 1928: Yesterday Judge Creed decided that Dr. Konikow was not guilty under the statute because in showing contraceptives to an invited audience of her patients and friends, she was not advertising or exhibiting in the legal sense of the words. I was delighted to see how much more sympathetic and open-minded the lawyers are today than they were ten years ago, when the subject of birth control was a source of acute embarrassment.

I feel cautiously optimistic now, for I believe that we have entered into a new era for birth control. The League has revived and redirected its energies: at our meeting this evening, we reached the decision to work solely on modification of the law in order to exclude physicians from its application.

In the meantime, we shall send notices of the trial and its outcome to the medical journals, the *Birth Control Review*, and *The Nation*.

<u>May 31, 1928:</u> About twenty-five attended the League meeting today to adopt a new constitution and discuss the best way to approach medical groups. Dr. Henry Stevens, formerly president of the medical association of Massachusetts, told us of the necessity for a permanent, active organization for education in birth control to cooperate with and stand behind those courageous doctors who would be willing to take the risk of giving advice to patients in spite of possible indictment under the law.

After the meeting Dr. Stevens told me privately that physicians also need us to educate them. Although the medical journals have begun finally to include discussion of birth control methods, doctors do not know much about them, and they are in the dark as to which are most effective. He was intrigued to hear about the occlusive pessaries made from condoms and rings, and when I offered my home for the instruction of physicians, he said that would be a great service to the profession.

Mrs. Sanger is wise to place finding the one simplest effective contraceptive at the top of the agenda for the American Birth Control League—I feel certain our eventual success will rest on that discovery.

<u>January 23, 1929:</u> Membership in the Birth Control League of Massachusetts has grown to sixty, and there are many more sponsors now. With a few hundred dollars in the treasury, we have engaged a halftime secretary. Progress is slow

but steady, except with the hospitals, which resist our efforts to introduce information about contraception there.

May 5, 1930: We have just engaged C. L. Carter to go out into the field and enlist support for the bill, which we hope the doctors will present to the legislature. A tiny office was rented and a full-time stenographer engaged.

January 3, 1931: Last Tuesday, December 30, Mr. Parkman introduced the Doctors' Bill to Clarify the Law in the state legislature; it was presented in the form of a petition for law, signed by fifteen prominent physicians. Signatures of thirteen hundred doctors, four hundred ministers, and seven thousand laymen accompanied the bill, and it was endorsed by the Massachusetts Federation of Churches.

The bill has been referred to the Public Health Committee. To garner support from women's groups and clubs, we are writing letters to the effect that the suffering of the mothers which this bill seeks to help is within the knowledge and sympathy of every woman; of all the legislation that has come up in recent years, this is the most vital to women—not vital in the figurative sense, but literally vital as a matter of life or death to hundreds of married women every year in the state of Massachusetts. During the last legislature more than fifty bills pertained to women and children, but none touched upon a woman's right to life itself, as this one does.

The Commonwealth of Massachusetts
House of Representatives
State House, Boston

January 7, 1931

Mrs. Del Easton
225 Ridge Way
Wellesley, Mass.

Dear Madam:

Your letter on Senate Bill #43 received and contents carefully noted. Personally I believe that you have a nerve to attempt to foster such a bill on the people of this Commonwealth. I am glad you brought same to my attention because now I'll take the floor of the house and denounce you in every way, shape, and manner for attempting to coerce me with such vicious propaganda.

I suppose that you are the type that prefers a *lapdog* for a companion.

Representative Herbert P. Shaughnessy

P.S. I will now get all my Protestant friends to vote against said bill.

February 6, 1931: For several weeks, physicians of the highest standing testified in hearings before the Public Health Committee concerning the medical need for giving contraceptive advice to save life or to cure or prevent disease. The opposition declared that passage of the bill would lead to widespread immorality, claiming that it would not be safe to entrust the right to give advice to the medical profession as a whole because the medical profession is of such a low order! They also asserted that the birth control movement is undoubtedly supported by Soviet gold.

Today the committee voted "leave to withdraw." I am so furious I don't know what to do. This is the work of Cardinal Olivetti and the influence of the entire hierarchy of the Roman Catholic Church—they have abandoned the women of this state once again. WHY DON'T THESE MEN MIND THEIR OWN BUSINESS!

As always, women must resort to their old expedient of self-help; mothers must teach their daughters how to regulate conception, since their doctors are not allowed to supply the means. I shall draw up an illustration of the way in which to make a device that will inhibit conception. At the bottom of the page, I will add the formulae for spermicidal jellies.

That's why Kate hated the Roman Catholic Church!

June 13, 1932: In February a group of physicians signed an appeal for funds to establish the Brookline Mothers' Health Office, an extramural clinic in which to introduce contraceptive advice and other health services needed by women. Women of means have always had doctors who will help them. Now we can get the same information to women who can't afford their own physician. The clinic is open and receiving patients under the supervision of the Medical Advisory Committee of the Birth Control League. Medical and social agencies and hospitals are referring more women every day. The League has started to consider opening a similar clinic in Springfield.

Cassie skips a bunch of pages. Then:

June 11, 1937: At last! The American Medical Association has finally endorsed birth control as a proper medical practice. Now physicians can prescribe contraceptives for the protection of the lives and health of mothers and children. This is a tremendous step forward.

August 8, 1937: The police came and closed down the Brookline Mothers' Health Office despite the fact that it has been recognized as one of the best in the United States, known not only for its high medical standards and the thoroughness of its work but also for the quality of sympathetic interest in each patient—a rare accomplishment for a clinic. When it was shut down by the police, eighty-eight medical and social agencies were referring women to avail themselves of its services. Every year approximately five hundred women were being directed to these Mothers' Health Offices or to physicians who worked in cooperation with the League to care for poor patients who could not afford to pay the usual doctor's fees.

Our clinics in Worcester, Fitchburg, Salem, New Bedford, and the South End in Boston were shut down as well.

This is an outrage! Who is going to take care of these poor women now?

October 4, 1939: This month's *Atlantic* includes an article by Father Francis J. Connell entitled "Birth Control: The Case for the Catholic." In it he states, "When husband and wife deliberately and positively frustrate the procreative purpose of sexual intercourse, they pervert the order of nature and thus directly oppose the designs of nature's Creator. And since the reproductive function is so vital to the upkeep of the race, and since any exception to this law would be

multiplied indefinitely, every act of contraceptive frustration is a gravely immoral act, or, in Catholic terminology, a
mortal sin." Later he states, "There is inevitably a lowering of
mutual respect between the husband and wife who agree to
make use of contraception."

October 7, 1939: I have finished writing a letter to the editor of
the *Atlantic* in response to Father Connell. It starts, "Careful,
Atlantic! Father Connell claims divine authority for birth
control condemnation." I go on about Pope Pius XI citing
Genesis xxxviii, the story of Widow Tamar and Onan. I talk
about science, and then I turn to the Pope's encyclical "On
Christian Marriage," which states "a wife's duties, primarily
of 'ready subjection' to marital rites, secondarily of 'the qui-
eting of concupiscence.'" I say that these duties, "combined
with the possibility of annual childbearing, place on her a
heavy burden. For many it means death. Often it means a
life of fear, a conflict of wrongs: whether to wrong her husband or wrong her children. If women use contraceptives,
the Church torments them by threats of eternal damnation.
Just as the abolitionists sought to free the slaves, so we,
speaking for millions of women, ask the Catholic Church to
follow the example of Saint Peter. He superseded the Jewish
commandment on circumcision by quoting Jesus—that the
Church concern itself with things spiritual, not physical. By
the same merciful inspiration, the Church should supersede
its birth control laws."

December 1, 1940: Finally home from attending the
Women's Centennial Congress in New York, the purpose of
which was to appraise one hundred years of women's progress and to chart the future. Birth control was excluded from

the preliminary program despite Margaret Sanger's request that the topic be included.

As a state delegate to the Congress, I was unaware of what had already transpired on the subject, but I succeeded in convincing the other members of the session on ethical and religious values to adopt a resolution that women should seek greater representation on the governing boards of the Jewish, Catholic, and Protestant churches "to the end that the point of view and religious opinions of women may be more directly reflected in Church creeds, and that tolerance and mutual respect for honest convictions may strengthen our democratic way of life and guarantee our religious freedom," indirectly linking this with birth control.

Finally, after a turbulent time getting the resolution into the final reports and distributed to all the delegates, one after another of Margaret Sanger's friends came forward, and the birth control issue was discussed.

To me and others who spoke up then, it seemed incredible that a Congress called to celebrate one hundred years of women's freedom and the righting of grave grievances should omit a full discussion and recognition of Margaret Sanger's organized, national effort, covering a period of approximately twenty-five years of constant education and legislative activity, to give a woman the freedom of choosing for herself the times she shall bear her children and the number she shall bear.

Yet the Congress itself dared not discuss the role which birth control has played in making it possible for women to emerge from their historic and ancient role as "breeders of men."

I will never forget the quiet smile with which Mrs. Roosevelt, who was presiding, slipped into her purse my written request to be heard in the full convention. She, too, believes in birth control, and she was politically wise about when to raise the subject.

Cassie lays down the papers. She is growing more and more convinced that she has found a promising topic for her dissertation. If she were to analyze the history of the Birth Control League of Massachusetts, it would be a real contribution to understanding the movement that was originally named by Margaret Sanger.

Then Cassie starts to think about the job opportunity Ann mentioned. The university's Social Welfare History Archives is advertising for a research assistant for a women's history project. That could be fascinating work, and it would bring her some income, which she sorely needs now. And where is she going to live? Ann said she could stay with her indefinitely, but it occurs to Cassie that she's never lived all by herself before and that it might be good for her to try. So many changes! Her head is spinning and she still feels weepy, but being able to think about the future must be a good sign. Perhaps she's stronger than she knows. In fact, Cassie is starting to realize that she could be a strong Reed woman after all.

CHAPTER 20

March 1978

The telephone rings in the middle of the night, startling Cassie awake. She reaches for the phone on her bedside table, afraid that a call this late means bad news. Scrutinizing the alarm clock, which shows 4:00 a.m., she says, "Hello."

"Cassie? It's Steven. We have a son! Paul Morgan Rose was born half an hour ago."

Her eyes fill. "You named him after Dad!" Blinking her tears away, she goes on. "That's great news! How's Penny doing?"

"She's just fine. Pretty tired—she was in labor for twenty-four hours."

"Oh no! And the baby?"

"He's healthy; his lungs are strong. Can you hear him crying?" There's a pause.

Faintly she can hear a sort of mewling sound in the background. "This is so exciting, Steven! I can't wait to meet him."

"When can you come visit?" Steven's so pumped up, she thinks he must be on the verge of levitating. Of course, he's excited about the birth of his son.

Then she feels a stab of regret, wondering how Martin might have sounded if he'd been announcing the birth of their child. Not that she knows much about Martin anymore. A few weeks after her abortion, she received a formal letter from him addressed to her in care of her mother in Norwich, who forwarded it to Cassie at Ann's. Martin wrote on his law firm's letterhead, asking her to provide her current contact information so he could initiate no-fault divorce proceedings. He went on to inform her that since Minnesota is one of the first states to allow no-fault divorce without having to prove adultery or cruelty, and because they have no children or significant shared assets, the divorce should be granted quickly.

On October first, when she moved into an apartment on the top floor of a duplex near the university, she called Martin at his office to give him her new address and telephone number. She'd hoped he would be friendlier than he'd been when she moved out of their house, but he responded as though he were speaking to a client. Coolly, he informed her that she needn't appear in court—he'd handle everything.

"What about Lucy?" she asked. "I want her to live with me, now that I've got a place of my own."

Martin said, "No. She stays with me."

"But you're gone so many hours of the day and night!"

"As you very well know, the house has a fenced backyard and a dog door. Lucy can come and go as she needs."

Since then a friend of hers who still works at Faegre and Whitney told Cassie that Martin was dating the new paralegal at the firm. *Already!*

Her mother doesn't understand why she and Martin are breaking up. Her explanation about wanting to be an independent woman didn't make sense to Liz.

"Sorry, Steven, I was just thinking. We have spring break at the end of the month. Maybe I can fly out to meet the baby then. I'll see if I'm able to get time off from my job."

"That would be fantastic! I know Penny is dying to see you."

"We were together not that long ago, for Christmas."

At Christmas when Cassie told Penny how lonely she felt, Penny answered, "The best way to get over a man is to get under another." She'd been startled by her sister's saucy reply. There's no way she's going to get under just any man.

"She's been worrying about you, Cassie, living on your own, all alone."

"I'm all right, Steven. Tell her not to waste her energy worrying about me."

"Well, I'd better make some more calls. Penny wanted you to be the first to hear our news."

"I'm honored and happy for you both."

After hanging up the phone, Cassie knows she'll never get back to sleep now. She might as well start her day.

While she showers, Cassie thinks back to December. Their first time without her father in the pulpit radiating joy at the birth of the baby Jesus—it was excruciating. They were all there: her mother and Nanny, Steven and Penny, and Matt. Everyone except Martin. Cassie missed him, though not nearly as much as she missed her father. Penny looked really good, all pink and glowing. Liz had done her usual festive decorating, they'd gone caroling in the hospital, and Cassie made her famous gravy for the turkey. Everyone tried to be cheerful, but Paul's unexpected death was still tough to digest.

Christmas Eve when they got home from church, Liz drank too much and Cassie had more than one snifter of brandy. As she climbed up the stairs to her bedroom, she caught herself lurching a little. She stopped at the telephone table on the landing, feeling desperately lonesome and sad. She really wanted to talk to Christopher. Guessing he would be at his parents' home, she picked up the receiver and started to dial the number she'd memorized years ago. Then she stopped herself, put the receiver back down in its cradle. She knew she should wait before she reached out to him.

By January the novelty of living on her own had completely worn off. She wasn't looking to find happiness right away, but she did hope to feel less depressed and empty. Now, whenever she recalls the dream she'd had about the life she and Martin were going to create together, it makes her cry. She thinks about him more often than she ever imagined she would. Receiving Helen's announcement of her daughter's birth wasn't easy either.

Sometimes Cassie feels as though her entire world has collapsed; her underpinnings have given way. She hadn't realized how much she relied on her father's love and her husband's support. What's left now? Other times she feels excited about making a fresh start as a single woman with resources of intellect and energy and education. Veering back and forth between these poles gets quite disorienting. Her one achievement in the last six months was passing her prelims— she's proud of that.

It's been months since she has slept really well. She doesn't feel like she has a real home any longer, but she tries to create some warmth by filling her apartment with plants and candles. She likes to cook, though. Buckwheat groats with tamari and broccoli with hollandaise is a favorite meal. When she needs cheering up, she makes a half batch of chocolate chip cookies for herself. Last week she went to the movies on her own for the first time, but she hasn't yet managed to eat by herself in a restaurant. Over dinner in her apartment, she always has a book by her side for company.

Nighttime and weekends and holidays are tough. Because she's lonely, especially at night, in bed, that's the time she allows herself to read novels. Right now, she's enjoying *The Realms of Gold* by Margaret Drabble, an engaging love story about a divorced archaeologist mother of four who's bored with her life. If she were pregnant, Cassie might not feel so alone.

Talking on the telephone with Charlotte has been helpful, but Charlotte may be losing patience with her because she sounded pretty gruff the last time they spoke. Charlotte told her, "You've got to take charge of your life. You must get to know yourself, Cassie:

what matters to you, what moves you. You've got to really *like* your-self. You need to get into such a relationship with yourself that you'll never feel lonely again." Good advice, but how the hell is she sup-posed to do that?

Fortunately, during the week Cassie's job as research assistant for the Women's History Sources Survey consumes her. The purpose of the project is to identify and document all the primary sources and organizational records pertaining to the history of women in America, which will be published as a reference resource for historians. The first challenge was to convince research libraries and historical societies and archives around the country to reconsider the materials in their possession, typically described in terms of the influential politicians, military men, and civic leaders whose documents they hold. Project staff had designed questionnaires to elicit the information they need, and for those repositories whose holdings were especially large or significant, the team hired graduate students in history to spend the summer as fieldworkers digging into those collections. Now the staff is at the stage of writing up the findings from the questionnaires.

Cassie's job is to verify all the dates and names. She's part of an impressive team of young women and one man who are passionate about proving that the actions and writings and thoughts of women and the positions they held, the organizations they created, the schools they founded, the causes they espoused, are just as histori-cally significant as those of men, even if they are less well-known. She really enjoys being part of this group.

Now that she's single, people seem to want more from her than they used to. Her mother often telephoned in the early evening after she'd had a few drinks, so Cassie finally told her to call in the morn-ing instead. She identifies with Liz's grief, but there's no point in talking with her mother when she's loaded. She feels relieved when her mother goes to Florida with Nanny for ten days because then she can stop worrying about her for a little while.

Penny had taken to calling Cassie every weekend with the latest report on her pregnancy, which Cassie did and did not want to hear. She struggles to separate her own feelings from those of her sister because she wants to be supportive.

Cassie also listens to her friend Ann, who goes on at great length about whether to be a lesbian or not. Ann believes that the only real feminists are gay. Cassie thinks that's ridiculous. Moreover, she isn't convinced that lesbianism is actually a matter of choice.

Despite the fact that Cassie knows her mother considers Valentine's Day an invention of Hallmark, she sent Liz a Valentine anyway, hoping she'd understand it was meant to indicate Cassie was thinking of her. Liz never mentioned receiving the card, but that doesn't matter.

These days, all Cassie's socializing is with single women. She doesn't have much time for anything besides her job. She's working forty hours a week on that project, and she really enjoys it, but she hasn't made much progress on preparing the research proposal for her dissertation.

She thought she'd write about how the Birth Control League of Massachusetts morphed into the Massachusetts chapter of Planned Parenthood, but when she met with her advisor two weeks ago, Dr. Nichols said that wasn't a meaty-enough thesis for a PhD. Dr. Nichols suggested that Cassie look at how grass-roots birth control groups developed in other states, which would enable her to contrast those groups' experiences with the particular challenges that the Massachusetts League faced in its struggle to survive. The prospect of so much additional research and travel before she can start writing makes Cassie feel absolutely sick. She almost considered giving up— she could settle for the master's degree she'd already earned—but then one morning when the sun came out after several gray days, more constructive ideas began to occur to her.

Meeting with her advisor last week, Cassie proposed comparing the evolution of the Birth Control League of Massachusetts with what happened in Minnesota. That way she would be able to readily access local resources for research. Dr. Nichols agreed with her plan, reminding Cassie that while she was lucky to have Kate's diaries as part of her review of the literature, she would also need to read a variety of secondary sources, like *Woman's Body, Woman's Right: A Social History of Birth Control in America* by Linda Gordon. Cassie has already read that book.

While Dr. Nichols's agreement is good news, this cold, dreary winter feels like it will never end. Perhaps she should get a cat.

CHAPTER 21

Philadelphia, Pennsylvania

During the cab ride from the Philadelphia airport to Penny and Steven's apartment in Center City, Cassie's spirits lift to see that tulips and daffodils are already blooming here. In Minnesota the ground is covered with dirty snow. When the cabbie stops, she hurries up the stairs, excited to meet the baby.

Once she takes the little bundle and settles him against her chest, she recalls what Kate intimated about holding baby Lucia in her arms. While Kate was comforting Lucia, her own heart was receiving some comfort as well. Cassie dips her head down to sniff the top of Paul's skull, which is covered with a remarkable amount of black hair. He smells so good. He feels wonderful. She looks over at Penny, who sits in an adjacent chair, smiling fondly at them both.

Cassie says, "My heart just wants to wrap itself around this little tiny boy. He is so sweet."

"He's an angel when he's sleeping," Penny replies.

Paul jerks awake and starts to fidget. His lower lip trembles. Soon he's crying louder than Cassie would think possible for a child this young. She bounces him in her arms, but he just cries harder. She feels a little nervous now; she doesn't know how to quiet him.

"Here," says Penny, "I'll take him." Standing, she leans over Cassie and lifts Paul up. "Shush, little one, Mommy's got you now." Sitting down, she rearranges the blanket around Paul. He settles down, closing his eyes again. She turns to Cassie. "He's not used to your smell yet."

Is that a whiff of condescension in Penny's tone? Or maybe Cassie simply feels defensive about not sharing motherhood with her sister.

"He's still so new," Cassie replies. "How does Mom like him?"

"Are you kidding?" Penny chuckles. "She's absolutely besotted."

"That's the impression I got from her," Cassie agrees. "She told me she stayed with you your first week home from the hospital."

"She was a great help, but after six days I was ready for her to leave us to ourselves."

"How do you think Mom's doing, Penny?"

"The baby's a great distraction for her."

Cassie remarks, "It must be wonderful for Mom to have something positive to think about."

"It seems to me Mom doesn't really know what to do with herself right now. I think she's really glad not to have to deal with the auxiliary any longer; that new minister's wife has taken over there. Mom's spending more hours in the soup kitchen."

"That's good."

Penny says, "Mom started talking about moving to Philly, but I told her not to do that. We don't know where Steven's residency will be."

"Did the idea of Mom moving here make you nervous?"

"Not really. She invited me and the baby to spend the summer at Granite Cove with her and Nanny. She said it would be very nice for Nanny too."

"Are you going to do that?"

"It's tempting—Steven is working so many hours he's hardly ever home. On the other hand, I wouldn't want us to be away from him for that long. We'll see."

"Can you play it by ear?"

"Of course," Penny replies. "I'm going to put Paul down. Stay put; I'll be right back."

"May I make us some tea, Penny?"

"Sure. You'll find everything in the kitchen."

As Cassie puts the kettle on and opens cupboards to find mugs and tea bags, she recalls a line that struck her while she was reading *The Women's Room* on the plane this morning. When her first child was born, the character Mira "felt she had arrived, finally, at womanhood." This seems to be true in Penny's case. Cassie senses that her sister has become a grown-up.

Once Penny returns, the sisters sit at the little kitchen table facing each other with their mugs. Penny asks, "How are you doing, Cassie?"

"Well, I can't afford to be sad right now—I have too much work to do."

"It'll catch up with you."

"Later. It turns out that I still need to do a lot more research for my thesis before I can start writing."

"What's it about?"

"I'm comparing and contrasting the evolution of the Planned Parenthood in Massachusetts with the one in Minnesota."

"Are they very different?"

"Yes. The Roman Catholic Church had a stranglehold on the politicians in Massachusetts. As a result, it took much longer to establish Planned Parenthood there."

"Hmm."

Penny doesn't sound all that interested—or maybe she doesn't know what else to say. "How are you feeling about everything, Cassie?"

"I still cry during the music at church. I've started attending Plymouth Congregational Church, where they have a fabulous choir. I feel close to Dad there."

"Do you ever regret your decision?"

"Which one?"

"To have an abortion?"

"No. No regrets about that. I'm so grateful I had the choice. If I didn't have control of whether and when to bear children, I wouldn't have control of my life. Being able to plan my own life gives me the freedom to dream."

"You're passionate about this, aren't you?"

"You bet I am! Have you ever thought about the fact that *any* woman who gets birth control and education can climb out of poverty and make a good life for herself? It takes both."

"I can't argue with that."

"While I was in the process of recovering from my abortion, it occurred to me that Mom really *did* want me."

"Of course she did."

"Sometimes I wondered. She seems so much happier with you."

"I bet being a good parent to your first child is much more challenging than caring for subsequent kids."

"That makes sense, Penny."

"Tell me, what's going on with Martin?"

"I don't really know, though I've heard he's dating someone. Last week I spotted him at a Saint Paul Chamber Orchestra concert—he didn't see me—and I realized then, I still have some residual feelings of love for him. That's really confusing. Occasionally I have regrets, but mostly I know I did the right thing."

"How do you like living on your own?"

"I love being able to eat whatever and whenever I want. Martin's a meat-and-potatoes guy, whereas I prefer chicken and fish. I can stay up as late as I feel like. And there's no one telling me what to do, how to go about my research, how to live my life. It's great!"

"What about Christopher? Have you been in touch with him?"

"No. I think I need to spend more time on my own, get over my fear of being alone, learn to enjoy my independence."

"That sounds smart, Cassie."

"Actually, I'm following Aunt Charlotte's advice. We've been talking a lot since last summer. She's the one who's wise. I'm dying to contact Christopher, but I know Aunt Charlotte's right when she says I should wait."

"Do you ever get scared living by yourself in an apartment?"

"I should feel safe, but I find myself double-locking the front door and checking the windows every single night. I don't like being alone so much when it's dark outside. That's when I feel lonely. Usually I read myself to sleep."

"Doesn't sound like much fun."

"At least I've got lots of time to work, and I'm motivated to finish my dissertation as soon as possible. I'll be coming east in July for some final research, and I need to return a packet of letters to Aunt Charlotte. I'm a little worried about her. She has a horrible cough that just doesn't seem to get better." Cassie takes a sip of tea. "Anyway, that's when I hope to see Christopher."

CHAPTER 22

Minneapolis, Minnesota

Cassie's boss sticks her head around the partial wall that shields Cassie from the other women working at their desks on the Women's History Sources Survey. "Cassie," Theresa says, "I'd like to see you in my office."

"Now?"

"Yes." She sounds very serious.

Uh oh. As Theresa turns and moves toward the front of the large open room, Cassie stands quickly and grabs a notebook and pen. Has she done something wrong? She feels a little scared that she's about to be fired. She needs this job.

Theresa is already seated when Cassie arrives. She says, "Close the door."

Cassie takes the chair facing Theresa, a woman with fiery red hair and a temper to match. She doesn't look happy.

"You've been doing excellent work here, Cassie. I appreciate your close attention to every bit of information that crosses your desk."

But . . .

"Thank you, Theresa. I really enjoy this project, and I love being part of the team."

"How is work on your dissertation coming along?"

"Slowly."

"I have to tell you, we weren't awarded the extension grant we applied for. I'm sorry, but I need to cut your hours, Cassie. I must cut your position down to half-time, starting next week."

"How will all the fact-checking be accomplished? There's still a huge amount of work to be done."

"I know. I plan to hire an indexer next month. The indexer can take over your responsibilities."

"In other words, before long I won't have a job at all?"

"I hope you can stay on long enough to explain our systems to the indexer."

Cassie replies, "I knew this was a temporary job, but I'm a little surprised that it's ending so soon."

"You'll have more time to work on your dissertation. That's got to be your top priority anyway."

"True." Cassie's mind starts to race. It has been awfully frustrating to make such snail-like progress on her thesis. Maybe this is a blessing in disguise.

Thinking aloud, she says, "Once I'm working half-time, I could spend the rest of the day going over the records of Planned Parenthood of Minnesota, which I know were recently transferred here from the Minnesota Historical Society. That would be good."

"Yes, that would be very good," Theresa agrees, nodding eagerly.

Cassie just has to figure out how she's going to be able to pay her bills. Should she move back in with Ann? She really doesn't want to.

Over the weekend, Cassie reviews her living expenses. Rent and utilities and phone and insurance and food total roughly $950 per month. Sunday morning, she telephones her mother.

"Cassie!" Liz answers. "I was just about to call you. Aunt Charlotte died yesterday."

"No! What happened?"

"She caught pneumonia about ten days ago. She went to the

hospital, but the doctors couldn't save her. I feel a little better know-ing her daughter, Nina, was with her when she died."

Closing her eyes, Cassie bows her head. After a moment she says, "I'm so sad. I was looking forward to seeing Aunt Charlotte again. And I borrowed something from her that I should return."

"Come spend some time at Granite Cove this summer. I'm sure Nina will be here dealing with the Studio, so you could give her what-ever it is that you borrowed."

"I'd like to come east. I really need to do more research at Smith."

Liz says, "Penny and baby Paul are coming for a few weeks in July and then again in August. Nanny and I would love to have you all—wouldn't that be fun?"

"It would. Turns out my job ends June 30."

"You could come for the whole summer!"

"No, I need to work on my thesis. But I was thinking, Mom, if I don't look for another job and just concentrate on finishing my grad-uate work, I could probably be done a year from now. I'd love to be able to do that, but I'd need to borrow some money from you."

"How much would you need?"

"I think eleven thousand dollars would cover my living expenses and travel costs."

"Let's call it twelve. I'll send you a check."

"Thank you *so much*, Mom. I promise I'll pay you back. I can't tell you how much this means to me!" She pauses. "How about you, Mom? I hear you're putting in a lot of time at the soup kitchen. I'm proud of you. That's really worthy service."

"Those who are hungry must be fed."

"Good for you. Aside from that, how are you doing?"

"I keep busy. I've decided to sell the house—"

"What? You didn't tell me you were thinking about that. Are you sure?" At this point Cassie considers the house she grew up in her only home.

"It's much too big for me to handle on my own." Liz sounds matter-of-fact, but Cassie knows her mother loves the house, with all the light it gets from so many windows, the cozy nooks for sitting, the larger spaces for entertaining, the gracious feel of the place.

"I wish you didn't have to, Mom."

"Same here, but my circumstances have changed."

"I know; I understand."

"I started going through the stuff in the attic, making piles for the Union Gospel Mission and Goodwill, throwing out twenty-five years' worth of junk. It's a big job."

"I bet. Please don't throw away any of the books in my old room."

"What do you want me to do with them?" Now Liz sounds annoyed.

"Could you make me a list, so I can tell you which I'd like to keep?"

"I guess I can do that."

"Great. Thank you for everything, Mom. I really appreciate all your help."

By the end of July, after spending a week on her research at Smith, Cassie arrives at Granite Cove. Penny and Paul have returned to Philadelphia for a week, and Liz is in Norwich looking for a new place to live because she's already received a good offer on the house, but Nanny is there to welcome her.

Her grandmother is in much better spirits than she was last summer. As they sit on the Bungalow porch over gin and tonics before dinner, Nanny says, "We had such a good time with Penny and the baby earlier this summer, and I'm glad that Penny's coming back next week. Paul is such a sturdy little fellow. Sometimes Penny lets me give him his bath—*that's* a big treat."

"Really?" This surprises Cassie. Somehow, she doesn't think of her grandmother as someone who loves infants.

"There's nothing so soft as the skin of a baby." Looking down at her lap, Nanny smiles to herself.

"I know what you mean, Nanny. I got to hold Paul when I visited them in March. He smells really good." For a second she remembers that she could have been holding her own baby in her arms by now, but then she pushes the thought aside. She's not ready to tell Nanny—or her mother—about her abortion. Maybe later when her decision doesn't feel quite so fraught.

"Now tell me all about what you're studying," Nanny says. She lifts her drink and takes a sip.

Cassie lights a cigarette before she speaks. "I'm looking at the organic similarities and differences between the development of the Birth Control League of Massachusetts and the Minnesota Birth Control League, which started off being called the Motherhood Protection League. They called it that so they wouldn't expose its real purpose."

"I suppose they had to do that."

"Both organizations set up birth control clinics in the early 1930s. The clinics in Minnesota continued uninterrupted except for one month, when they were short of funds, but the clinics in Massachusetts were shut down by the police after five years."

"I don't remember hearing about that."

"Aunt Kate must have been so frustrated, even though she was no longer president of the Birth Control League of Massachusetts at that point. She still kept up the fight in other ways."

"She was a tough one."

"A strong Reed woman, as Aunt Charlotte would say."

"Charlotte . . . " Nanny sighs, then turns her head to stare out at the ocean.

"It must be awful to lose your sister, Nanny."

Nanny returns her attention to Cassie. "It is. I miss Charlotte, especially here."

"I bet you do. I'm so sorry she's gone."

Nanny picks up her glass and takes a sip.

Cassie asks, "Have you seen Nina?"

"I had tea with her yesterday. She's been sorting through her mother's papers. That reminds me. She said she'd found an envelope with your name on it. You should go call on her."

"I'd like to. I assume she's staying in the Studio."

"That's right. Give her a call now; see if she's available tomorrow morning."

"I will."

The next day, Cassie walks over to Charlotte's house. As she stands outside the open front door, she hesitates a moment. She doesn't want to believe that Charlotte won't be here.

After knocking on the frame of the screen door, she waits. A thin woman with long dark hair and Charlotte's eyes appears.

"Yes?"

"Nina? I'm Cousin Cassie."

"Come in," Nina cries, flinging open the door.

"You look like your mother!" Cassie responds. "I'm so sorry about Aunt Charlotte. What a wonderful woman! I'd just started getting to know her this past year."

"She enjoyed her conversations with you. Let's sit down." Nina looks around the room, where all the chairs are stacked with books, papers, and files. "Let me clear a place for you." She removes the piles on two adjacent seats.

Cassie settles on the spot Nina indicates. Nina sits facing her.

Holding the letters Charlotte had loaned her last summer, Cassie says, "I have some things you might want. I promised to return these to your mother."

"What are they?"

"Old letters between Aunt Kate and Del Easton that your mother found in the desk here when she bought this place."

Nina says, "Keep them if you like. I wouldn't have any use for them."

"Really?" She's surprised that Charlotte's daughter wouldn't have any curiosity about old letters her mother had saved. "Well, thank you. Have we ever met before?"

"Maybe a long time ago. I live in Seattle, and I don't get back east very often."

"This place is so charming—what do you plan to do with it?"

"My brother wants the Studio. He lives in New Hampshire, so it's not such a trek for him." She stands and walks over to the desk. "Now, where did I put that envelope with your name on it?" She starts moving around the papers on top. "I know it was here some-where." Finally, she retrieves the envelope from under an etched glass paperweight.

Cassie reaches out. Charlotte's hand must have been very shaky when she inscribed Cassie's name on the front. Turning it over, Cassie sees that it's been sealed. She can hardly wait to see what's inside. She gets up, thanks Nina again, and leaves.

When she returns to the Bungalow, it isn't until Nanny goes upstairs for her nap after lunch that Cassie opens the envelope from Charlotte.

There's a cover note that says: "My dear Cassie, I saved this for you, but I didn't think you should receive it until after you'd decided what to do about your pregnancy. I didn't want this to have any impact on your decision. I believe Aunt Kate wrote these words as a way to purge herself of a terribly painful experience. It's such an important part of her history that I want you to have it. My love to you, Aunt Charlotte."

Kate's handwriting covers the pages inside.

Paris, 1911

Absolute darkness—fathomless—impenetrable—darkness. Then slowly, gradually, I started to emerge from the depths of unconsciousness, dimly aware that someone was shaking me—"*Levez-vous, madame, vous devraiez vous lever et partir à l'instant!*"[1]—no, too sleepy—like a feather I floated back down the well. Some time later, I wondered where I was. At the sound of a metallic instrument clattering onto the floor in the next room and then a muffled "*Merde!*" I began to remember the stench of urine that pervaded the stairwell and the sordid stairs I mounted, the gory smock of the doctor as he leaned down to place the chloroform-soaked cone over my mouth and nose.

As I exhaled, the cloying pungency of the anesthesia threatened to suffocate me again. My senses swirled, and then I was overwhelmed with nausea.

Gagging, I frantically pulled myself into a sitting position while someone shoved a basin at me. When the bout of retching finally subsided, I gazed groggily at the sooty sheet that covered the small window. I wanted to die. Then my nostrils were assailed by another noisome odor, and I discerned what appeared to be a smear of fecal matter along the side of the basin in my lap. I retched some more.

Once my stomach was empty, I became aware of the burning in my pelvis; it felt as though a hot poker in my belly was jabbing at my guts again and again and again.

Although I was gasping with pain, the attendant pulled me off the bed, hurried me into my clothes, and dispatched me down three flights of stairs. I struggled into the waiting carriage, whose progress over the cobblestones was so jarring that after trying to hold myself rigidly upright, I slid to

---

1 "Get up, Madame. You must rise and leave immediately!"

the floor, where I propped myself up on stiff arms so that my knees, not my midsection, absorbed the jolts. In this pathetic posture, a feeling of utter humiliation swept over me. This was the first time since childhood I had experienced such a sense of debasement, but I cast it aside; I could not allow myself to notice anything but the physical agony right then.

Finally I reached the sanctuary of my room. I lurched forward, thinking I should undress, when a wave of dizzying pain mounted and crashed down upon me, drowning the dregs of my defenses. I cried, "Mother, oh, Mother, help me. I'm scared. It hurts so much. Make it stop. Please, Mother. Help." Whimpering, I crawled over to the bed, hauled myself up, and then I collapsed. Soon the bedclothes beneath my body blossomed with blood.

Later, I was hazily aware of someone removing my clothes and putting some other garments on me. Although I was rolled to one side of the bed and then the other as the bedclothes were changed, I was barely aware of this.

. . . Cold, so cold . . . shudderingly cold . . . the sticky wetness that seeped from me was sucking all my heat out.

. . . Much later—it must have been another day, I thought, for I could see the light behind my closed eyelids—I heard a deep voice saying, "*L'avortement n'est pas complet . . . complications septiques . . . retention placentaire . . . l'hémorragie . . . curetage.*"[2]

A voice I recognized, shrill with outrage, expostulated, "No! This can't be true. You must be mistaken, Doctor."

"*Mais non,*" the doctor replied. "*L'infection . . . mesures plus radicales . . .*"[3]

---

2 "The abortion is not complete . . . complications with sepsis . . . retained placenta . . . hemorrhage . . . curettage."

3 "No . . . infection . . . more radical measures."

I sank back into unconsciousness.

Many hours later I awoke to a blindingly white hospital room. All the pain and fever were gone, but I felt totally empty. My body stretched out on the bed like a vast plain.

Cassie covers her face with her hands. As she compares Kate's ordeal with her own, tears slip out from between her fingers. Then her heart fills with gratitude for Planned Parenthood.

CHAPTER 23

Granite Cove, Massachusetts

Once Nanny goes to bed for the night, Cassie telephones Christopher's house. Her hands are shaking as she inserts her finger into each hole to turn the rotary dial. While the phone rings and rings, Cassie wonders what she would say if he has one of those new answering machines. Finally, Christopher picks up.

"Hello."

"You're there, Chris! I was hoping you would be."

"Cassie! How are you? *Where* are you?"

"I'm down at the Bungalow with Nanny. May I come up?"

"It'll be good to see you." He sounds a little cautious. The last time they saw each other at her father's memorial service was pretty awkward, and there's so much he doesn't know about what's been going on with her since then.

Cassie quickly changes out of the dress she was wearing for dinner with Nanny and puts on her new cuffed short shorts and Take Back the Night T-shirt. Then she hurries up the hill, her heart pounding hard. The full moon makes it easy for her to navigate through the trees and shrubs. A cloud suddenly covers the moon for a moment but quickly passes by. Lights shine from the distant shore. She spots a lightning bug and then another. This has got to be a good sign.

When Christopher opens the door, heat rises in her chest. He shifts aside to let her enter.

They stand facing each other. She wants to hug him, but suddenly she feels shy. He might have gotten engaged since last summer.

Smiling, he says, "You look wonderful."

"So do you." His face is lightly tanned, which intensifies the nearly navy blue of his eyes. His sideburns aren't quite as long as they were last summer.

"Still The Same" is playing on a nearby radio. She says, "Bob Seger."

"Yeah, good song. Can I get you a beer?"

"That would be great."

While he leaves for the kitchen, she scans the room for any signs of a female visitor or co-inhabitant. Spotting none, she relaxes a little. She takes a chair adjacent to the couch and picks up the copy of *War and Remembrance* lying facedown on the coffee table.

When he returns and sits on the couch, she asks, "Do you like this book?"

"Yes, very much. Have you read *The Winds of War*? It comes right before this one."

"No, I haven't."

"I think you'd like them." Leaning forward, he puts his elbow on his knee. "Tell me, how are you doing? I bet you miss your father terribly."

"I do. Christmas was awful. But Penny and Steven had a baby in March, and they named him after Dad."

"Cool! How's your mother?"

"Mom's smitten with baby Paul, which helps cheer her up. And she's selling the house. That's a little hard, though it makes sense."

"It sounds like she's doing pretty well, considering."

"I agree. What about you, Chris?"

"I'm still at the Massachusetts Public Interest Research Group. The work continues to fascinate me."

"I'm glad for you."

"How is the work on your PhD going?"

"It's coming along. I was just at Smith doing more research on how the Birth Control League of Massachusetts evolved to become an affiliate of the Planned Parenthood Federation of America in the early 1940s. But I'm feeling kind of confused. Last night I was reading Linda Gordon's book about birth control in America again—more closely this time. She said the Massachusetts Birth Control League was led by socialists. Maybe it had something to do with the accusation that the movement was funded by Soviet gold. But that's not the impression I've gotten—it's hard to believe my Aunt Kate was a socialist."

He leans back. "Why would you say that?"

"How could Kate be a socialist when she and Del came from families with money?"

"Presumably she developed her own opinions and values."

"What about you, Chris? What does it mean to be a socialist if you come from some money and you have a professional degree, a good job? I really want to understand."

"I give all I can give and take as little as I can. I'm frugal. I don't buy fancy stuff. I give a lot of my income away. And I do pro bono legal work every week."

"That's all good." She still feels a little nervous, so she takes a big gulp of beer. Then she continues. "You know, it is so complex. Women's thinking about birth control is complicated by their differences in class and race and the consequences of those differences over generations. There's so much to study and think about. I'm going to have to do a lot more work before I can actually start writing my dissertation."

He frowns a little. "Are you all right, Cassie?"

"The truth is, it's been a hell of a year. Dad's death."

"Of course."

"And then I had an abortion."

"Whoa, that can't have been easy for you."

"It wasn't. Martin and I got divorced soon after." Now she feels completely vulnerable and really scared. *What if Christopher doesn't feel the same way I do?* She inhales deeply, then plunges in. "So, are you dating anyone these days?"

"No, I'm not."

"Would you ... possibly ... ever ... be interested in getting together with me?"

He replies, "Come over here."

She perches next to him on the couch. He reaches for her and pulls her close. As he holds her tight, she feels his heart racing just like hers. "It's you," he murmurs.

Foreigner's "Feels Like The First Time" comes on the radio.

She pulls back to look into his face. "Really?" She starts to tremble.

"You've always been the one for me."

He kisses her softly and then more intently. Her lips swell, and she feels her body opening to him.

She leans back. "I'm looking for more than a roll in the hay, Chris. I want a serious relationship."

"I do too." His eyes are so sparkly now. "Let's give ourselves a chance to see what can happen with us."

"Yes! There's no rush. I need to finish my dissertation."

"It'll have to be a long-distance relationship for a while, won't it?"

"But we can talk on the phone and write letters to each other. Will you come visit me in Minnesota?"

"Of course."

"So we'll see."

"Yes, we'll see."

Grinning hugely at each other, they hug again.

Later that night, Cassie discovers an illuminating entry in Kate's diaries.

<u>December 15, 1941:</u> The war has inspired me to join the corporation of the New England Hospital for Women and Children, to which I have given financial support for two decades, although I have had no personal involvement until now. I offered the hospital president my crucifixion painting. While the agony depicted there would not be appropriate for the patients' wards, I suggested that it might be welcome in the boardroom, and once Mrs. Burton had seen *The Crucifixion of Women*, she accepted my painting with enthusiasm.

This is a great honor. The New England Hospital for Women and Children is the first hospital in New England to be staffed entirely by women physicians. It was the first in New England to admit women as interns. It organized the first school of nursing in the United States, and it was the first hospital to admit a colored woman for training as a nurse; Adelaide Mahoney graduated from the School of Nursing in 1879. It was the first to start social service work, when a committee of three Boston women volunteered to visit the homes of patients known to be in need of friendly advice. It was the first hospital to hold evening classes to teach the care and handling of babies to new fathers.

I cannot imagine a more appropriate final resting place for this painting.

CHAPTER 24

The next morning on her way to go grocery shopping for Nanny, Cassie stops at the Gloucester Book and Stationery, where she finds the perfect notebook filled with empty, lined pages. After lunch, when Nanny retires for her nap, Cassie moves into the living room, places her Coke and cigarettes and pen on a nearby table, puts the notebook on her lap, and sits in a comfortable chair. She looks out at the ocean for some time, then picks up her pen, opens the notebook to the first page, and begins to write.

July 31, 1978

I want to start a diary of my own to reflect on this past year and organize my thoughts and observations. It could be a good way for me to learn more about my essential self.

As a female, I've always felt like a second-class citizen, despite the advantages I've had. Is it because I was taught that my role was to serve my parents, my sister, my brother, my husband? Martin didn't respect me when it came down to it. Did I kowtow to him too much when we were married? Maybe that's why he was shocked when I stood up for myself and insisted on what I wanted in my life.

Perhaps Mother felt like a second-class citizen too. Is that why she felt she had to accept what Fate brought her? Of course, that meant my birth, which I certainly don't regret. But she didn't have any real, safe alternatives. She had no way out of carrying me to term. Kate must have felt trapped as well.

If a woman doesn't have control over whether and when to have children, how can she have any control over her own future?

I'm terribly grateful to have been born into Mother's family, a family of strong women – especially Kate. But I don't have to follow in my mother's precise footsteps, not in Nanny's, not in Penny's.

I'm incredibly lucky to have found Kate. Kate respected herself. I don't believe she thought of herself as second class. She called Del on his thoughtless behavior when he didn't help her that time Lucia had pneumonia. Yet she held on tight to him when he was ready to give up on their marriage. She faced and overcame so many obstacles and challenges.

Kate dreamed about using her art on behalf of suffrage and then she went about executing political cartoons. She believed in herself and in causes that helped to liberate women.

I choose to emulate her. Kate inspires me to dream my own future.

Actually, anyone can choose who she wishes to emulate, who she finds inspiring, whatever dream she longs to pursue.

Now's the time for me to grab hold of my inspiration, my aspirations, my self-worth, to pursue my own path.

HISTORICAL NOTES

The diary entries in this novel were written by me, and though most of the characters mentioned in the diary entries are based on real people, I did not use their real names. In other words, the diary entries are largely fictitious, though they are based on actual historical incidents, especially those that pertain to the Massachusetts Woman Suffrage Association, the Birth Control League of Massachusetts, and the New England Hospital for Women and Children.

On the other hand, I have quoted verbatim from a few historical documents: President Taft's criticism in the September 11, 1915, issue of the *Saturday Evening Post* about the cartoon "Meanwhile They Drown"; the letter Massachusetts Representative Herbert Shaughnessy wrote dated January 7, 1931, to Mrs. Oakes Ames; and the diary entry dated October 4, 1939, where the fictional character Kate quotes an actual article in the *Atlantic* by Father Francis J. Connell. Blanche Ames Ames's reply to him was printed in the January 1940 issue of the *Atlantic*.

The letters between Kate and Del and the letters between Mrs. Easton and Mrs. Richardson are largely quoted verbatim from actual letters between Blanche and Oakes Ames and from exchanges between Blanche and the head of the Birth Control League's publicity committee, but I deleted extraneous material and made Del an expert on ferns rather than orchids.

The Ames Family Collection in the Sophia Smith Collection at Smith College includes suffrage cartoons created by Blanche Ames, sketches of a woman on a cross, correspondence between Blanche and Oakes Ames, and information about the New England Hospital for Women and Children. Smith College has provided permission to quote from these items in the Ames Family Collection.

Other information concerning the New England Hospital for Women and Children came from the Blanche Ames Collection at The Arthur and Elizabeth Schlesinger Library on the History of Women in America at Radcliffe College and from the New England Hospital for Women and Children Collection at the Nursing Archives at Boston University's Mugar Memorial Library.

The Crucifixion of Women

Sophia Smith Collection, Smith College

THE NEXT RUNG

Sophia Smith Collection, Smith College

Acknowledgments

This novel is for my daughter and all the other women born after *Roe v. Wade,* who don't know what it was like to face an illegal abortion at the hands of a butcher, and for all those older women who do remember.

There are many people I would like to thank for their inspiration, information, help, and support over the years I spent on the manuscript. They include Gary Hugh Phelps, Heather Huyck, Barbara Sheldon, Terry Sheldon, Sallie Sheldon, Marylee Hardenbergh, Louise Miner, and Sally Power.

Thanks to Sara Evans, Regents Professor Emerita, University of Minnesota, for her insights on the relationship between the civil rights movement of the 1960s and the women's movement of the 1970s (*Personal Politics: The Roots of Women's Liberation in the Civil Rights Movement and the New Left,* Alfred A. Knopf, 1979). I am most grateful for her thoughtful teaching and friendship.

Thanks to Roger Paine for creating a wedding service that I have cribbed from.

Thanks to Harriet Robey, Jim Rutherford, and Abe Sheldon for their ideas about the characteristics of the women in the Ames family, which underlie the discussion of Reed women.

I am deeply indebted to Erika Guenther and Connie Guenther for their insights.

Thanks to Jay Howland, Gayle Graham Yates, George Hage, Ron Hubbs, Saudimini Siegrist, John Sweetser, Alan Burns, Lyn Cowan, Mary Logue, Maggie Gluek, Susan Weil, Ron Hansen, and Oakes Plimpton for their thoughtful reading of early drafts.

Thanks to host Roger Barr and the other members of our writers' group—to Cynthia Kraack, Charlie Locks, Loren Taylor, Jim Lundy, Terry Newby, and Kathy Kerr—for their support and comments.

And thanks to fellow author Lynn Abrahamsen for her savvy strategic thinking and to Angie Weichmann and Betsy Williams for their sharp editorial eyes.

Allison McCabe, a brilliant developmental editor, made great contributions to the manuscript. In addition, I am very grateful to Brooke Warner for creating She Writes Press, a cutting-edge hybrid press, and to editor Lauren Wise, and cover designer Julie Metz at She Writes Press. Thanks, too, to my publicist Jackie Karneth of Books Forward for helping me reach a variety of audiences.

Sarah Stoesz, President and CEO of Planned Parenthood of the North Central States, and Dr. Jennifer Childs-Roshak, CEO and President of Planned Parenthood League of Massachusetts, have been hugely important partners in helping to get this story out.

And my profound thanks to Andy, the staunchest supporter of all.

About the Author

© Brad Stauffer

Ames Sheldon is the lead author and associate editor of the monumental reference work *Women's History Sources: A Guide to Archives and Manuscript Collections in the United States*, which taught her to love writing about the history of women in America. She is the author of two award-winning historical novels with strong female protagonists. *Eleanor's Wars* won the 2016 Benjamin Franklin Gold Award for Best New Voice: Fiction. *Don't Put the Boats Away* won in the Family Saga category of the 2020 American Fiction Awards, and was a finalist in the 2020 International Book Awards, National Indie Excellence Awards, Next Generation Indie Book Awards, and the 2019 Best Book Awards.

Sheldon comes from a family of ardent supporters of reproductive rights for women.

An alumna of Bryn Mawr College, Sheldon lives with her husband in Eden Prairie, Minnesota. Follow her at www.amessheldon.com.

SELECTED TITLES FROM SHE WRITES PRESS

She Writes Press is an independent publishing company founded to serve women writers everywhere. Visit us at www.shewritespress.com.

Don't Put the Boats Away by Ames Sheldon $16.95, 978-1-63152-602-2
In the aftermath of World War II, the members of the Sutton family are reeling from the death of their "golden boy," Eddie. Over the years, they all struggle with grief and pay high prices, including divorce and alcoholism, but they develop resilience, too.

Just the Facts by Ellen Sherman $16.95, 978-1-63152-993-1
The seventies come alive in this poignant and humorous story of a fearful rookie reporter at a small-town newspaper who uncovers a big-time scandal.

Magic Flute by Patricia Minger $16.95, 978-1-63152-093-8
When a car accident puts an end to ambitious flutist Liz Morgan's dreams, she returns to her childhood hometown in Wales in an effort to reinvent her path.

Shrug by Lisa Braver Moss $16.95, 978-1631526381
It's the 1960s, and teenager Martha Goldenthal just wants to do well at Berkeley High and have a normal life—but how can she when her mother is needy and destructive and her father is a raging batterer who disdains academia? When her mother abandons the family, Martha must stand up to her father to fulfill her vision of going to college.

The Moon Always Rising by Alice C. Early $16.95, 978-1-63152-683-1
When Eleanor "Els" Gordon's life cracks apart, she exiles herself to a derelict plantation house on the Caribbean island of Nevis—and discovers, with the help of her resident ghost, that only through love and forgiveness can she untangle years-old family secrets and set herself free to love again.

Again and Again by Ellen Bravo $16.95, 978-1-63152-939-9
When the man who raped her roommate in college becomes a Senate candidate, women's rights leader Deborah Borenstein must make a choice—one that could determine control of the Senate, the course of a friendship, and the fate of a marriage.